HOPELESS

BOOK 2
OF

Λ VISION OF VΛMPIRES

By Laura Legend

Hopeless. Copyright © 2018 by Laura Legend. All rights reserved under International and Pan-American Copyright Conventions. By payment of the required fees, you have been granted the nonexclusive, nontransferable right to access and read the text of this e-book on screen. No part of this text may be produced, transmitted, decompiled, reverse-engineered, or stored in or introduced into any information storage and retrieval system, in any form or by any means, whether electronic or mechanical, now known or hereafter invented, without the express written permission of the publisher.

Cover art by Momir Borocki

First edition

EPub Edition September 2018
Print Edition September 2018

ISBN: 9781723768170

Printed in the United Sates of America

For Buffy and Faith, my favorite badass vampire slayers

1

THE SUN WAS slow to rise over the ridge of the mountain and flood the valley with light.

An ancient Zen monastery, repurposed centuries ago, was tucked firmly into the deep shadows at the mountain's base. A single light shone behind a single paper door on the highest floor of the compound's oldest building. Inside, Kumiko Miyazaki was angry.

"Cassandra Jones," Kumiko angrily whispered. "Cassandra Jones. Cassandra Jones." She repeated the name like a mantra. Each time she repeated Cassandra's name, she said it more quietly and more angrily until her eyes glowed with just a hint of green.

A quiet Kumiko was a dangerous Kumiko.

Kumiko's lieutenants were gathered in the room at a low, Japanese table. The room was lit by a lantern. Water for tea was near boiling. They sat with their legs crossed, their hands in their laps, and their heads bowed. They occasionally stole a sideways glance at each other but carefully avoided eye contact with Kumiko.

When Kumiko finally trailed off into silence, Dogen, her chief lieutenant, risked a response.

"Master," Dogen said, hesitating. Dogen shifted his bulk nervously and bumped the low table that, next to him, looked like a tiny, ridiculous toy. The cups rattled in their saucers. He rubbed the bridge of his flat, acne-scarred nose in a gesture of apology. "To be fair, Jones isn't our real problem at the moment. Our real problem is the Lost. Jones cut off their head when she defeated Judas and, ever since, the Lost have grown more wild and ravenous." Finished, he bowed his head in deference and his pony tail bobbed.

"No," Kumiko said, gathering her sleek, modern kimono more tightly around her and drawing herself up to her full height. At 4'10" she could almost look Dogen in the eye when he was seated and cowed. Still, she seemed to tower over him. "Our real problem is that the Lost, rather than being headless, have—with alarming speed—been brought to heel behind a new leader."

She paused, scanning their faces for reactions. "I need to know," she said, clipping each word short for emphasis, "who their new leader is. And I need to know *now*."

Her voice descended into a whisper again until everyone at the table sat perfectly still. She deftly removed the teapot from the heat and began pouring, with great precision, the same amount of tea—exactly—into each lieutenant's cup. Her straight, white hair was coiled into a bun and pinned in place with a deadly looking needle. A small, brown fox curled between her legs and disappeared under the table.

"I've served as your leader for hundreds of years. I've worked tirelessly to gather and conserve the power we would someday need to shield the world from the Lost. And, in all that time, we've *never* faced the kind of deep instability outside that threatens us now."

The tea was scalding hot. No one dared touch it.

"Do we have any information about who their new leader is?" Kumiko hissed. "Anything?"

Silence.

Kumiko gently set the teapot back in its place. She turned back to the table, her eyes narrowing.

"Get out," Kumiko whispered, pointing at the door. "Get out and don't come back until you have something to report."

The lieutenants all glanced, simultaneously, at their just poured tea.

"No tea for you, today. Out!"

The whole group stood at once and filed toward the door. Dogen, though, was a touch slow and a touch clumsy. He bumped the table again, rattling more china and spilling tea. He glanced at Kumiko, shrugged, and tried out a tiny, apologetic smile.

"You," Kumiko said to Dogen, "sit back down. We have something else to discuss."

Dogen sighed loudly and sat down, trying not to show that he was secretly pleased to stay.

Kumiko could read him like open book. She glanced at her strong but wrinkled hands, then smoothed an errant strand of white hair back behind her elegant ear. She didn't look a day over eighty. Now, though, was not the time. She would continue to ignore the fact that Dogen had (with little success at concealing his unspoken feelings) pined after her for years. Sometimes this was flattering. Sometimes this was inconvenient. But sometimes it was useful.

"Dogen," she said, trying out his name and a softer tone of voice. "I fear that we've been betrayed. I fear that those we've trusted most have proven themselves . . . unworthy of that trust." She reached out as if to touch his hair, but stopped short and let her hand fall back to her side.

Dogen bowed his head and cocked it to one side in a gesture that signaled both curiosity and a willingness to agree. His arms were the size of most people's thighs. His stomach rumbled. He glanced at his tea.

Kumiko followed his eyes to the tea.

She snapped her fingers to get his attention. "Dogen," she said, "I need you to find out if our worst fears are well founded. I need you to bring home our wayward sister—by force if necessary—so that we can determine how desperate our current situation is. She may be the only one who knows for sure who is now leading the Lost. And, worse, she may well be implicated."

Dogen gulped but nodded his head. Then his eyes again settled longingly on his tea.

"Fine," Kumiko sighed, "drink it already."

Dogen pinched the handle of the tiny teacup between his massive fingers and lifted it to his lips. The tea was still scalding hot. He hesitated and glanced up at Kumiko.

"Go on," she said, waiting. "Drink it already." Kumiko's fox slipped out from under the table and darted for the door.

The whole cup of tea disappeared in Dogen's mouth in a single sip. His mouth burned and his face turned red. Kumiko cocked an eyebrow when he looked like he might spit it out, so he swallowed the mouthful in one go.

"Now gather a handful of soldiers that you trust and be off. Be back as quick as you can. And *do not* let her slip through your fingers. Do whatever is necessary."

Dogen swallowed again. "Yes, master," he said, his answer slightly slurred by his burned tongue.

"Whatever you do," Kumiko whispered, "don't come back without her."

2

CASS FELT HOPELESS.

Or, at least, she felt herself feeling hopeless.

She felt hopeless in that frustrating way that, since her mother's death, she'd tended to feel all her emotions: one step removed, as if she were watching herself in a movie. She could sense her emotions knocking around inside of her, locked up behind a heavy wooden door, but she couldn't *quite* feel the emotions themselves. This made her own life feel distant and alien and, often, it made her feel powerless. Recently, though, since she'd met Richard, the lock on that door seemed to be weakening.

At the moment she could sense the approach of that same swelling hopelessness that, for months now, had been sneaking into her apartment each night to squat like an anvil on her chest, squeezing the air out of her until she could hardly breathe. Remembering Richard didn't help: the hopelessness mixed with a sense of loss that throbbed steadily against her sternum, striking a seemingly empty space, reminding her that something important, some possibility not yet realized, was simply gone. Missing.

She was stretched out on the old leather couch in her studio apartment in Salem, Oregon. It was after two in the morning. She was exhausted but couldn't sleep. She rubbed her temples with her thumbs. Her breathing was shallow and thin. She wondered where Atlantis, her orange tabby, was. She hadn't seen him in weeks.

She tried to think about something else, anything else—work tomorrow, Zach, Miranda, her dad—but, this time of night, like water circling a drain, her thoughts always came back to the same thing. Her thoughts always circled back to those last few, climactic minutes in Judas's castle. Again and again, she would find herself stuck in a loop, running through the events of that night in her mind, over and over, looking for things she might have done different—until finally sleep would claim her for a few hours before dawn.

But it didn't matter how many times she resurrected the events of that night, it didn't matter how many times she relived that nightmare, things still ended the same way.

She still lost Richard.

Tonight was worse than normal. A deep headache was growing in the back of her head, throbbing up from behind her weak eye, pulsing with a regular rhythm that made her head feel like it was going to split open. She clapped her hands against the sides of her head as if to keep it from coming apart. She willed herself to contract her attention to the tight, tiny circle of her shallow breath, in and out, here and now. She willed herself to treat the thought of anything beyond her next breath as if it belonged to another life in another world.

It started to work. Her breathing slowed, deepened slightly, and she slipped toward something like sleep as the hopeless pressure in her chest eased.

Then, suddenly, the weight and pressure returned, worse than before. It planted itself on her solar plexus and grew heavier and heavier. She tried to open her eyes, but couldn't. Everything was black. She felt herself being sucked down into the cushions of the couch, pressed down under the growing weight of her pain. She felt a black void opening up beneath her. Her hands scrabbled for something to hold on to, clinging to the edges of the couch frame. But it was too late. She lost her grip and was swallowed by darkness.

She fell.

She fell slowly for a long time, watching herself fall, watching the faint light from her apartment recede into a small square framed from the inside by the edges of her couch, watching until even that light disappeared altogether. Then, in total darkness, she felt only the weight on her chest carrying her downward, faster and faster, together with the sensation of endlessly sinking.

Just when she thought she might fall forever, she smacked into the surface of a hard, stone floor. And the lights came back up. She knew immediately where she was. In fact, she knew immediately *when* she was. She was back in Judas's castle in Romania. She was going to relive that night again.

She tried to move, to take action, but her feet were blocks of cement.

Her aunt and best friend were tied up and unconscious in the corner of the room. She tried to call their names, to wake them and warn them—"Miranda! Zach!"—but no sound came out.

Cass could see that, as always, she and Richard were chained to chairs in the center of the room. An enormous fire raged in the fireplace at one end of the space and Judas was assembling his "crown" from fragments of the One True Cross at the other.

Judas was giving his monologue again, droning on about how the crown would empower shadows like him to wander freely in the light, their darkness spreading across the world like a drop of black ink in a glass of clear water, until the whole world became a shadow of itself.

From across the room, Cass watched her former self struggle uselessly against the chains that bound her. She watched Judas, enraged by the fact that one crucial fragment of the Cross was still missing, attack Richard with crackling tongues of white-hot lightning. She watched herself scream for Judas to stop. And then, finally, she watched Judas discover the missing fragment of the Cross hidden in the amulet that her mother had given her years before, just before her death.

With the missing fragment in hand, Judas rose from the castle floor in a swirling cloud of power and light. Richard lay on the floor, his broken body smoking.

No, Cass thought to herself, just offstage. *Not this time. Not again, you piece of shit.*

She gathered her strength and broke free of the inertia that, for months now, had cemented her in the corner of the room as a tortured observer. She stepped into the light of the still-unfolding scene. She saw Judas drawing the power of the Cross into himself. She saw herself still chained to the chair and Richard still sprawled on the floor. And she saw Zach and Miranda still bound in the corner.

But when Cass tried to step entirely into the light, the shadows themselves came to life and reached for her. A hundred shadow hands with razor-sharp shadow claws emerged from the darkness and snagged her arms and pinned her legs. Cass stumbled to her knees. The hands multiplied and their claws hooked into the flesh of her arms and legs and dragged her back toward the darkness.

No, no, no, Cass thought.

She closed eyes and set her jaw.

I . . . said . . . no!

Deep behind her weak eye, a small flame flickered to life and, like a match to gasoline, her whole body was abruptly engulfed in white flames, burning the shadows away.

"Not this time," she said, finding her voice, speaking aloud. "Not again."

Cass sprinted for her katana on the workbench behind Judas, dodging debris from the roof that had already begun to collapse around them.

Judas turned and looked straight at her, surprised. He looked at the other Cass, still in chains in the chair. And then he looked back at her, sword now in her hand, and cocked an eyebrow at her.

"This is a surprising turn of events," he said. "But you're still too late."

He was right. The castle was already coming apart. The roof was still collapsing.

"Screw you, Judas," Cass spat as she turned her back on him, letting him go, and—this time—she ran instead for Richard. Giant blocks of granite rained down around her. She slid under one, dodged another, and with a running swing split a third clean in half with her sword as it was about to crush Richard.

She dropped her sword and it clanged to the ground. She gathered Richard in her arms, his tattered shirt still smoking, but he was too heavy to lift. His eyes fluttered open and met hers.

She kissed him on the forehead.

"Cassandra Jones," he rasped.

"I'm sorry, Richard," she said, kissing him again. "So sorry." And it was true. She was sorry. She knew she was. She was, perhaps, more sorry than she'd ever been about anything—even if she couldn't quite feel it.

Just then, the remaining crush of the roof collapsed, coming to bury them . . . and Cass woke up with a start, back on her couch. She felt like someone had just used a defibrillator on her. Her face was wet with beads of cold sweat and streams of hot tears. She wiped them both away with the back of her hand and sat up on the couch.

She tried to gather herself. She pulled her straight black hair back into a ponytail. She leaned forward, her head in her hands. Her eyes were ringed by deep black circles.

That was different this time, she thought. *At least it was different. For once, we were together at the end.*

Cass shivered, goosebumps running up and down her thin, strong arms. She was only wearing shorts and a camisole. She stood up and looked around the room for something warmer to put on. She usually kept a blanket on the back of the couch.

Looking back at the couch, she didn't find a blanket. But she did see a piece of black fabric poking out from the corner of a couch cushion. She leaned in, studying it, and pulled it free.

A silky pair of men's underwear. She'd never seen them before in her life. But they did look *really* expensive. She couldn't help but think of Richard. She couldn't help but imagine that he had a whole drawer full of bespoke underwear just like this, each of them monogrammed with his initials.

That wasn't helpful. She needed to stop this. She needed to let him go.

She neatly folded the boxers into a small square and tucked them back into the cushions of the couch. She strongly suspected that she'd never see them again. As she did, the sun peeked over the eastern horizon and slanted weakly through her bay of windows.

She stared at the cushions on her couch for a long time in the morning light. She stared for so long that she started to feel like she was falling again.

That couch was weird. There was no denying it. And it always had been.

She shivered again and tried to assess the situation. Part of her wanted to check. *Was* there anything under those cushions? Was there just a vast emptiness waiting beneath their cracked leather, waiting to swallow her up? But the other part of her just wanted to toss the thing onto the street and buy a Barcalounger instead.

She held her hand out over the couch and swore she could feel a draft of cold air coming from beneath the cushions.

Cass bit her lip and steeled herself. She took hold of one corner of one cushion and lifted it up just enough to steal a look underneath. An impossibly black abyss seemed to yawn open beneath the cushion. She dropped the cushion and backed away.

Shit. Have some guts, Jones, she taunted herself.

She steeled herself again, took two steps forward, and was about to reach for the cushion a second time when a heavy hand pounded on her apartment door, rattling the whole door in its frame.

3

CASS SILENTLY SLIPPED past the many wooden arms of her wing chun practice dummy and into position next to the door, snagging the modified version of her mother's katana from the kitchen counter as she did. She calmed her nerves and settled into a fighting stance, sword raised.

The pounding came again.

She waited without answering.

Whoever was in the hall turned the knob back and forth, rattling the door, testing it, but the door was dead-bolted in three places.

Cass took a deep breath and held it.

"Cass, I know you're in there," Zach called. "You've barely gone out in weeks. Open the door already!"

Cass deflated like a balloon, releasing the air she'd held in her lungs. She'd have cut him in half if he'd come through the door. She was relieved. And, then, embarrassed. She *had* been keeping to herself and she *had* been avoiding Zach. She wasn't sure if, even today, she could handle seeing him.

"Cass," Zach called again, his voice muffled by the door.

She still didn't respond.

"I brought bagels and coffee," Zach baited her, his voice much softer, as he rattled the paper bag in his hand.

Cass hesitated. Then her stomach rumbled, loud enough to be heard on the other side of the wall—when was the last time that she'd eaten? She slid back all three deadbolts in one motion and swung the door open.

"That's my girl," Zach started to say, still standing in the door, but stopped mid-sentence when he saw her standing there, barely dressed, sword in hand, with deep black circles under her eyes.

"Cass—"

Zach gently shut the door and put the bagels and coffee on the counter. Cass kept herself at an angle to him so that she wouldn't have to meet the concern in his eyes. How could she explain any of this to him? How could she explain any of this to herself?

Zach sat on a barstool and took her hand, gently pulling her toward him. He reached to take the sword out of her hand but, without meaning to, she recoiled, and almost nicked him with the blade.

She backed up a couple of steps.

"Alright," Zach said. "Why don't you hang on to that thing for a minute while we settle in."

Zach circled the island of counter space that separated the living room from the kitchen and opened a bunch of cupboard drawers looking for clean plates. Nothing. The sink, though, was full of used plates. He pulled two small plates from the pile, let the tap water warm for a moment, wiped them clean, and set them out with bagels.

"Sorry," Cass said, pulling up a barstool. She ventured a smile.

Zach beamed back, his smile as wide and crooked as ever. He ran a hand through his black hair. The morning light flattered his dark complexion. He slipped off his leather jacket and, in a t-shirt and jeans, pulled up his own barstool.

Zach took a small bite and then watched Cass, in two quick bites, devour half of hers.

"I brought coffee, too," Zach said, "to remind you that we both have jobs. At the same place. At a coffee shop. And Java's Palace isn't the same without you." He paused. "And from what I can tell, it will definitely *be without you* from now on if you call in sick again. Today is a non-optional workday."

Cass hung her head and stuffed the rest of the bagel into her mouth. She chewed slowly, her cheeks full of bagel.

Zach took another bite of his own, his bicep flexing in the tight t-shirt.

Cass raised an eyebrow. "Have you been working out, Zachary Riviera?"

Zach blushed. "No," he said. "Maybe a little."

She waited.

"Fine," he confessed, "I've had a lot of time to myself while you've been locked up in here. Time to train and reflect. And repeatedly lift very heavy things with my arms. Over and over. Not thinking about you. At all. What was I supposed to be doing?"

Cass smiled and punched him in the arm. He started to protest but saw an opening and switched gears.

"Now you owe me," he said, grimacing and rubbing the sore spot on his arm. "And you're going to have to leave the apartment to make it up to me." He looked her in the eye. She lasted for a couple of seconds and then looked away.

"I don't know how to do it, Zach," Cass said, tossing her plate into the sink with a crash. "I don't know how to go back to living a normal life. I barely knew how to be normal before I learned that the world was filled with vampires and that I'm . . . whatever it is that I am." She could feel the crush of hopelessness constrict her breathing, bringing her up short. She rested her hand on the pommel of her sword, reassured by the weight and balance of it.

Zach put his hand on top of hers.

"You weren't *meant* for normal, Cass," he started. "You were never meant to live a normal life." He squeezed her hand. "But that doesn't mean that you weren't meant to *live*. You still get to have a life. It will just have to be . . . an abnormal one."

His tone was dead serious but his eyes sparkled with mischief.

Cass tried hard not to smile.

"Believe it or not, my life hasn't been especially normal either. You've seen enough to know that I'm not exactly the feckless barista you may have thought I was. I've seen things, Cass. Like you, I've done things that I can hardly believe myself. But at the end of the day, we're still just people. We still have to sleep at night and shower and use the crapper. We still have to eat bagels."

He pulled her reluctant fingers free from the hilt of the sword and then set the sword aside on the counter. Cass's eyes followed it there. Zach took her chin and pointed her face at him. He looked straight into her weak, wandering eye.

"Come back to us, Cass," Zach said. "Come back."

That direct appeal was more than Cass could handle. She fell forward into him, squeezed back tears, and hugged him fiercely.

I need this, she thought. *I need someone here. Alive. Human.* As much as she believed her own words, she still couldn't help but wonder what it would have been like to have Richard here giving her this talk, this hug. *Come on Jones,* she told herself. *Zach's the one who always shows up. Let him.* Cass tightened her squeeze.

Zach, unaware of her internal conflict, held her for a long time, drinking in the scent of her and not kissing the nape of her neck, until she whispered in his ear: "Okay."

"Excellent!" Zach exclaimed, holding her at arm's length and tugging the strap of her camisole back into place. "Now, the first order of business," he continued, pinching his nose shut, "is to get you into the shower."

He spun her around and marched her in the direction of the bathroom. She playfully complied.
"Fine," she said, taunting him. "A shower it is."

And with that, Cass stepped into bathroom, turned her back to him, pulled off her camisole, set the hot water running and the steam rising, and, with the back of her foot, only partially shut the bathroom door.

4

IT MIGHT HAVE just been the lighting in Java's Palace, but Cass could have sworn that, for the rest of the day, Zach blushed whenever they bumped into each other behind the counter.

She felt a little guilty about it—while she showered and dressed, she could hear Zach reading the newspaper in the other room with an extraordinary level of intensity and focused attention, sometimes clearing his throat, sometimes slightly repositioning himself on the couch to emphasize that he was *not* looking in the direction of the half open bathroom door—but she didn't feel so bad that she wouldn't do it again. She liked to see him squirm.

They were busy in the café all day. It felt good to settle into the easy rhythm of taking orders and making espressos. A couple of times, Cass even caught herself laughing and smiling. Zach was right. She did need to get out of the apartment. She needed to just *live*, even if she didn't know where that living was headed. If she could manage to show up for her life, the business of living might take care of itself.

Before Cass knew it, it was late in the afternoon. The sun was already low in the winter sky when, in a dramatic swirl of gusting wind and dead leaves, Miranda pushed through the door and into the café. Her eyes flashed green and crackled with life. She looked stunning in her slim pantsuit and heels. Every face in the café turned and watched her walk to the counter.

"Finally," Miranda said, taking Cass's measure, noting how the circles under Cass's eyes were balanced, for the moment, by the lingering hint of a smile. She reached out and took Cass's hand, holding it in both of hers. She turned it over, palm up, and studied it for a moment as if she were going to tell her fortune. She traced Cass's lifeline with the tip of her finger. "Just what I thought," she mumbled to herself. Then, abruptly, she kissed Cass's palm, winked at her, and, nodding toward the door, said: "Let's go."

The clock chimed five. Cass's shift was officially over. Cass hung up her apron. She smoothed her frayed t-shirt and tightened her ponytail.

Zach, pretending not to watch the two of them preparing to leave, made a comically sad face.

"Fine. You, too, Riviera," Miranda said. "Meet us out front. Pronto." And then she swept back out the door in as dramatic a fashion as her entrance.

Zach smiled his crooked smile, hung up his apron, and vaulted over the countertop to catch up with Cass. But before they got to the door, he took Cass by the arm and pulled her to a stop. A look of horror passed over his face. "Wait," he said, "does this mean that Miranda is going to be driving us?"

Miranda, they both knew, was a terrible driver. Her sudden stops and starts, skids and turns, were enough to test even the strongest bonds of friendship-maybe-turning-into-something-more.

Cass gave him a blank and innocent stare, like he was a kid refusing his turn on the merry-go-round.

"Right. Maybe I'll meet you there?" Zach ventured.

"Come on, you chicken," Cass said. "You can't just 'meet us there' because you don't even know where we're going." This time she took *him* by the arm and they shuffled out the café door.

Miranda was waiting, double-parked and already revving the engine.

Zach looked at Cass with pleading eyes.

"Shotgun," Cass said, adding salt to Zach's wound.

After Zach had finally finished folding himself into the tiny backseat of Miranda's red Audi TT, Cass slipped into the front. Before her door was even shut Miranda had floored the accelerator, burning rubber. The car snapped into action before, almost immediately, Miranda slammed on the brakes. Zach's feet ended up in the air as they stopped for a red light on that same block.

Zach scrambled to get his seatbelt on. He closed his eyes for the rest of the trip, occasionally peeking out between his fingers when the car drifted around a corner and Cass squealed.

They parked crooked in front of a karate "dojo" in a nondescript strip mall on the edge of town. Cass knew the place. She glanced at Miranda and smiled. Miranda slipped a hand behind Cass's neck and pulled her forward until their foreheads bumped together. "I know what you need," Miranda said, squeezing Cass's neck. "I'm here for you."

The dojo was worn, battered, and quiet. A Tongan fellow sat at the counter in the back. He nodded his head in their direction when they entered, then went back to whatever he'd been doing on his phone. Miranda led them past the man, through a door into the back that said "Do Not Enter," and then down a flight of stairs into the basement.

Something inside of Cass did cartwheels when, at the bottom of the stairs, the smell of sweat, leather, and month-old gym socks hit her. It was like she'd come home.

The basement was disproportionately large to the strip mall above. It was filled with mats, training equipment, and sparring rings. The space was lit by strong fluorescent lights that buzzed and, occasionally, flickered. Nearly a dozen fighters and trainers were working, scattered around the space. Nearby, a pair of fighters were sparring. Mixed marital arts.

Miranda claimed a bench, unzipped a gym bag, and handed both Cass and Zach some gear to change into. This was not the kind of place that had private locker rooms. And it was also not the kind of place where anyone cared. They slipped into their gear right at the bench.

"Go warm up," Miranda said, dismissing Zach. "I'll call for you in a few minutes." Zach gave her a mock salute and padded off in the direction of free mat.

Miranda ran Cass through a preliminary array of Tai Chi poses. Cass could feel her body waking up as her muscles remembered what to do. It felt good to be back. Cass had trained here for years, often participating in the (literally) "underground," invitation only MMA tournaments that were frequently held down here.

Cass couldn't quite remember how she had originally found this place, but it had been a godsend. She'd needed what it offered. She'd thrown herself into training and fighting. She did both with ferocity and dedication. She loved the way the focus and pain of the fight could cut clean through the emotional fog that, in the normal course of her day, kept her feelings at arm's length. She didn't mind feeling the pain of being hit—in fact, she almost liked it. She just liked being able to *feel* something, even if that something hurt. In all, Cass had spent more than a decade down here. She knew what she was doing.

"Better," Miranda grunted, holding the heavy bag as Cass unleashed a flurry of punches. "You look better. You look comfortable, at home."

Cass smiled and threw a wicked roundhouse into the bag that rocked Miranda backward.

"But you can't be comfortable anymore," Miranda continued, her voice taking on an ominous tone, "because this isn't a game anymore. You can't be comfortable because the world isn't what you thought it was. And, especially, you can't be comfortable because *you* are not who you thought you were."

Cass stopped, head bowed, sweat dripping, and tried to catch her breath.

"You are *the Seer,* a once in a century gift. And Seers, by definition, don't get to be comfortable."

Miranda took a deep breath, braced herself against the bag, and pressed her point.

"I've known for years that this day would come for you, though I didn't think it would arrive as explosively as it did. I'm sorry about that. I'm sorry I didn't do more to prepare you."

Miranda paused, searching for words.

"I've known for a long time about how the world was, about Judas and the Lost, and I trained for decades in the magic arts to be prepared for terrible moments like that. Your mother and I trained together. And during those years we took a solemn vow to do everything in our power to shield the world from the worst of that terror. Your mother was better than me, stronger than me. I've done the best I could, but I haven't always fulfilled that vow. And I definitely haven't always fulfilled that vow in the way my superiors wanted."

Cass glanced up, hungry for more of this backstory, but Miranda quickly brought the conversation back to Cass.

"But at least some of this wasn't my fault. Your situation is complicated in ways that my bosses don't appreciate. And it's also complicated in ways that *you* are not yet in a position to understand and appreciate. And, so—especially given your father's insistence that I keep my distance—I erred on the side of patience and caution with you. I kept it simple. I mostly kept quiet. And I mostly stayed on the sidelines of your life. That may not have been the right approach. We won, last year, but barely. And look how much it cost us."

Cass couldn't help but think of Richard. At the same time, something bothered her. This wasn't the Miranda she thought she knew. *Her* Miranda was filled with a quick energy and sharp wit; *her* Miranda would have apologized by taking her out for a night filled with irresponsible drinking. Or irresponsible anything. This Miranda, however, seemed to bend, burdened by an unknown weight. Who was she?

"We almost lost everything. We almost *all* died." Miranda's voice trailed off. "So, again, I'm sorry."

Then again, near death can change people, Cass reasoned. But she didn't know what to do with that kind of apology.

Complicated? she thought to herself, reflecting on the tangled ball of yarn that was now her life. *Ya think?*

But she didn't say it out loud. Instead, she launched into another flurry of punches, a spark of dark anger and black hopelessness fueling her blows. She hit the heavy bag faster and harder, faster and harder, until the dark leather split down the side and a blizzard of white stuffing flew out.

Miranda let go of the bag, coughing as she waved away the gently floating cloud of debris and picked bits of stuffing out of her hair.

Just as fast, all that black energy drained back into Cass's feet. "I'm sorry, too," she said sheepishly.

"I can see that," Miranda replied, then looked over her shoulder for Zach. "Let's go, Riviera. We're ready for you."

Zach raised an eyebrow at the split heavy bag and the swirl of stuffing floating to ground.

Miranda had them gear up for some friendly sparring and ushered them into a hexagonal MMA ring. "Let's go," she said, "let's see what you've got."

Cass and Zach circled each other. Zach shuffled his feet, playful. Cass just tried to stay on her toes, quiet the thousand questions in her mind, and recapture at least a modest amount of focus before Zach tagged her with a punch to the face.

"You know how to fight," Miranda said. "You've always been good at that. But this is different now. As the Seer, your powers run much deeper than you know. It's not just about the body anymore. And it will take years of training and experience before you can bring many of your powers into play. Beyond your natural athleticism, your powers as a Seer are grounded in your ability to be truthful. As the Seer, you can 'see' the truth in a given situation and, if you can respond truthfully, if you can accept the truth, then your actions will be rooted in a power that is much deeper than the strength of your own muscles and bones."

Zach took advantage of the fact that Cass's attention was divided between himself and Miranda. He playfully tagged her once in the side of her face and then swept her leg out from under her, sending her tumbling to the mat.

Zach smiled his crooked smile, ready to tease her about it. But before he could say anything, Cass had already popped up from the mat with a dark look in her eyes.

"Whoa, tiger," Zach said, his gloved hand outstretched, "easy. We're just playing here."

Cass shook her head, trying to clear the fog.

Miranda continued. "It will take time to explain how this works and even longer for you to feel your way into actually understanding it with both your mind and your body. And, to be honest, there may be much of it that can't be taught and that you'll just have to figure out on your own as you learn how to trust yourself and see the truth about yourself."

Cass feinted a punch and Zach danced away to the left.

"But, for the moment, take this as a guiding thread: at bottom, the truth about the world is that everything with a beginning has an end. The truth about the world is that everything passes. The rock bottom truth about reality is *time*. And, as a result, all of your powers are grounded in learning how to deal truthfully with time, with both the costs of time and, especially, the *power and potential* of time."

Cass could feel her weak eye twitching into focus in response to what Miranda was saying. She had noticed already that, when her powers kicked in, they depended on her being truthful and, more, that they tended to involve time slowing down. When this happened, it felt like time, normally closed and inevitable, had relaxed, opened up, and offered her space to act.

In response to her dark look, Zach had backed off a bit, waiting for Cass to make the next move. Feeling time open up a bit in this same way, Cass feinted a punch to Zach's ribs and then, before he could recover, caught him with a roundhouse kick that clocked him in the nose, sent a spray of blood across the mat, and knocked him flat on his back.

Cass felt a surge of power. And she liked how it felt. Or, at least part of her did. Because, at the sight of Zach's blood, the other part of her felt ashamed.

She was tempted to bury the first feeling beneath the second, to bury the joy of that power beneath her shame, but sensed that this would be the wrong thing to do. She sensed that, if she did that, she'd make things worse. She would, in a real way, be lying to herself.

She dropped to her knees next to Zach. He was already pinching his nose and trying to make a joke about how he really needed to stop hitting her foot so hard with his face. In her heart, Cass tried to acknowledge the truth of both feelings—both the power and the shame. She tried, in light of them, to bring Zach himself into focus.

Miranda watched with keen interest from the side of the ring. She looked like she was watching both the fight between Zach and Cass and the fight inside of Cass herself.

"That's right," Miranda said. "Don't run from it, Cass. Let the truth be whatever it is. Let your feelings be whatever they are. Don't bury them. See the truth of them. Your feelings don't have to stay locked up behind those heavy doors. You weren't the one who put them there in the first place."

I wasn't the one who put those doors there in the first place? Cass thought with alarm. *What is Miranda talking about?* Who *put them there?*

When she thought this, time slowed to a crawl for Cass. Sound dropped out altogether and a profound silence took hold.

Cass looked at Miranda. Then she looked at Zach. Everything came into incredibly sharp focus. She looked at the spray of cherry red blood on the mat. The blood came into focus as the outline of a flower, as several flowers—as a spray of cherry blossoms.

A memory of cherry blossoms welled up from somewhere deep inside her and bloomed in her mind. Her muscles went slack and Cass slumped onto Zach's chest.

The room went fuzzy. The sharp scent of blossoms filled the air.

Cass was seven years old. She was holding her mother's hand. In Japan.

5

CASS WAS SEVEN years old. She was holding her mother's hand. Her hand was dry and warm and strong. Rose Jones was wearing a white blouse and pink pedal pushers. The breeze was warm. The sun was high in the bright morning sky. Rose smiled at Cass and gave her small hand a squeeze.

They were in Nagano, Japan, at a cherry blossom festival.

Cass's dad was there too. In relation to little Cass, Gary Jones seemed impossibly tall and impossibly young. He was wearing brown chinos and a dark blue polo. Cass was standing between her parents. Pulling Cass close, Gary leaned over her head, whispered something in Rose's ear, and kissed her mother on the cheek. Rose laughed and smiled. Though he was raised mostly in the U.S., Cass's father was deeply Japanese in appearance and demeanor. Here, in Nagano, with Cass's mother, he seemed happy and at home in a way that Cass couldn't remember ever seeing.

A warm breeze stirred and blossoms fell like snow around them. Cass pulled free of Rose's hand and joined their dance, twirling like she was a flower spinning through the air, until she, like the blossoms, fell to the earth, dizzy and giddy.

When she looked up from the ground, Cass noticed that someone else was with them, too. A tiny, older woman in a kimono-like jacket with white hair pulled back into a bun and held in place with a pin: Gary's aunt.

The white haired woman pointed out some auspicious features of the blossoms, commented on the weather, and gave Rose's bicep a friendly squeeze. It was clear that, though she was Gary's family, she was here for Rose. Her bond with Rose was obvious, substantial, and grounded in something deeper than the coincidence of a family connection.

The morning was perfect in its simplicity.

Cass was filled with a rush of simple, uncomplicated joy at the scent of the cherry blossoms, the feel of the dark soil between her fingers, the sun filtered through the tree branches, and the presence of family. She popped back up from the ground, twirled again, and started to weave her way in and out of the trees, her arms outstretched.

She realized, with a jolt, that, in this memory, her feelings were entirely her own. Nothing was held at arm's length. There were no heavy doors with imposing locks. She just felt, simply and directly, whatever she was feeling. People made sense. *She* made sense. She let out a "whoop" and her mother, pausing mid-conversation with the older woman, laughed out loud at the sound of it.

Cass felt free, unbounded. She ran and ran, in and out of trees, in circles and figure eights, in widening gyres around her family until she lost track of exactly where they were. She stopped to listen for the sound of their voices. She was breathing hard and leaned against a tree.

A cloud passed in front of the sun and a shadow slanted across the ground toward her. She could see it coming. When it arrived, the shadow was cold and her skin, glistening with sweat, grew clammy. Goosebumps crawled up her arms, across her shoulders, and up the back of her neck.

Cass shivered. A creeping fear grabbed her.

The cloud darkened and spread and the sun was more firmly blotted out by its passing. Cass spun in a panicked circle, looking for some sign of her parents. She ran from tree to tree, looking for the light.

"Mom!" she called. "Mom!"

The black shadow followed her through the trees. The warm breeze died. The air grew colder still. The tree branches stopped swaying. The leaves stopped rustling. The birds stopped singing.

Cass started to run. Faster and faster. As fast as her little legs could take her.

The shadow was still coming.

She tripped over a tree root and fell. She skinned her hands and knees. The shadow was gliding across the earth, swallowing everything in its path. Cass tried to call out again, but she couldn't find her voice.

The shadow swallowed her.

All the color drained out of the day. And then the anger and fear drained out of her, too. A heavy door slammed shut inside of her and the blessed sense of emotional intensity that had saturated the memory was gone. Instead of feeling like a seven year-old, bubbling over with the hope and promise of life, she now felt almost thirty, bruised by life, barely hanging on to her second-hand emotions by a thin thread.

"Mom," Cass croaked, her voice weak.

Silence.

"Mom!" Cass cried.

A voice from behind her responded. "I'm here, sweetie," Rose said.

Cass looked up. Rose took Cass into her arms, pulled her into her lap. She wiped away Cass's tears and smoothed her hair.

"Shhhh," Rose said. "It's okay, now. It's okay."

Cass circled her arms around her mother's neck and squeezed hard, pulling her close.

"Cass, I need to tell you something. We don't have a lot of time. And I need you to remember what I say. Can you promise to remember?"

Cass sniffed back more tears and nodded her head against her mother's shoulder.

"I'm going to give you a magic word. Remember it. Keep it safe. And you can use it whenever you feel afraid. Just whisper this word to yourself. Think of me and then say it three times."

Cass nodded again.

"Are you ready? The word is *kibo*."

"*Kibo*," Cass repeated to herself, pressing it into her mind like a stamp into wax. "*Kibo*."

"That's right," Rose said, her eyes flashing green. "You've got it. Now hang on to it. It's an old Japanese word. It means *hope*."

Hope, Cass thought as the word cut through the fog of that memory, drawing her out of the past and back toward the present. Cass, though, didn't want to leave the memory just yet. She couldn't bear to let go of her mother again already. She squeezed harder and hung on to her mother for dear life.

"But what if I don't feel any hope. What if all I feel is . . . hopeless?" Cass asked, breathless. "What do I do, Mom?"

Rose pulled back and took a look at Cass. She held Cass's head between her hands and took her measure, looking deep into her eyes, like she knew that she wasn't talking to a seven year-old anymore.

"Hope isn't something you can have by yourself," Rose said. "Hope isn't something you can have all alone. It's something that can only be shared. That's why, when you say the word three times, you have to also think of me."

The cloud was gone. The sun was out. The warm breeze stirred again.

Rose brushed the dirt off of Cass's knees and took her hand.

"Are you ready?" Rose asked. "Should we go find your dad?"

Cass nodded.

Then the memory started to fade around the edges. Everything started to go fuzzy. And the sharp smell of sweat and leather filled the air.

But it wasn't over yet. Not quite.

Just as the vision was fading out, just as Cass was about to lose hold of her mother's hand, that hand—so warm and firm a moment ago—turned cold and slippery and shadowy. And just as she lost her grip on that hand, Cass's palm was nicked by the trailing edge of a razor sharp claw.

Cass woke with a start to find herself back in the gym. Zach and Miranda were bent over her. They shouted with relief when her eyes opened. They tried to help her up.

"Just give me a moment," Cass said, trying to remember what her mother had said, trying to make sure that it was planted deep inside of her where she wouldn't be able to forget it.

"*Kibo*," she whispered to herself, rocking back and forth,"*kibo, kibo*."

Zach was smiling down at her. "Let's go champ. Are you ready? Give me your hand," he said. Cass reached out to take his hand but stopped halfway.

The palm of her hand was cut and slick with blood.

6

CASS WAS WRUNG out by her experience in the gym, both the fight and the memory. She was emotionally and physically running on empty. She didn't tell Zach or Miranda what had happened. Even if she'd wanted to, she didn't know how.

She wiped her bloody hand on her shorts, accepted Zach's hand up, and pulled her street clothes back on. Miranda dropped her off at Java's Palace so that she could get her car. Cass headed straight for her beat-up Volvo parked behind the café.

All she wanted to do was go home and sleep.

It was late in the evening now. The streets were mostly empty. Halogen street lights flashed overhead as she merged onto the freeway. She tried to focus on the road. But, out of the corner of her eye, she kept seeing groves of cherry trees, just off the freeway, popping with white blossoms. She ignored these mirages and wondered if there would be anything to eat in her fridge when she got back to her apartment. It had been awhile since she'd gone shopping.

Cass drove on like this, her head barely tethered to her body, until she pulled off the freeway, parked her car, and got out to find that she hadn't driven back to her apartment at all. Instead, she'd driven *home*, to her father's house in the suburbs where she'd grown up.

When she realized what she'd done, she almost turned around and got back into the car. Her relationship with her dad, already tense since she'd bombed out of her doctoral program and lost her job at the university library, was as fragile as ever. He'd tried for years to keep Miranda away and Cass safe from being exposed to that crazy world of magic and vampires. And now Cass was in the thick of it, up to her neck in magic and vampires, queen weirdo herself.

Cass didn't know how to talk to him either. She didn't know where to start. She wasn't even sure how much he did or didn't already know. They'd never talked about any of these things. Her father could barely mention Rose's name without his mouth going dry and his throat closing up. Almost twenty years later, that wound was, for him, still open and weeping.

And now, a big part of Cass wished that her dad *had* succeeded in keeping her free of that world.

Cass stood in the driveway, hesitating about whether to go in. It was late enough—after nine—that her dad might have already gone to bed. He liked to get up early. But her decision was made for her when she heard a loud crashing sound. She peeked around the side of the house and saw that the garage light was on.

The string of softly spoken, but distinctly audible, Japanese curses that emanated from the garage made her smile. He was in the garage. And even if she wasn't sure that he wanted to see her, *she* needed to see him.

They'd never parked their cars in the garage. From the time they'd moved in, they only used it for storage. It was full of boxes of books, memorabilia, and who knows what else her father had squirreled away. Cass wiped her sweaty palms on her jeans, grabbed the handle to the garage door, and gave it a pull. The door swung upward, groaning on its tracks.

Gary's head was buried in a pile of boxes. In response to the creaking of the garage door, his head swiveled around, all the blood startled out of his face. When he saw that it was Cass, his face lit up for a moment, like a warm light buried deep in his heart had flickered on, like he was a lantern illuminated from the inside out. Then he recovered himself, remembered that he and Cass hadn't really been talking, and offered her a more distant, "Hello, Cassandra."

"Hi, Dad," Cass said. "What are you doing out here?" Cass toed the side of a box, titling it to see the handwritten label on the side: ROSE'S SUMMER CLOTHES.

"Ummm, nothing," Gary tried. "Nothing in particular. Just . . . rooting around."

A small box, balanced precariously on a tall stack, toppled and lightly bounced off the side of his head, disheveling his salt and pepper hair and setting his thick glasses askew.

"Uh huh," Cass said, craning her neck to read the label on another box: CASSANDRA'S TEA SET. "I see."

"What are you doing out here tonight?" he asked, a touch too sharply. He frowned at himself and added, his tone softening: "It's been a while."

Cass chewed on this for a minute, trying to decide what to say or how to start. She crossed her arms and rubbed her shoulders. Her breath plumed in the cool night air.

"I was thinking about Mom," she said.

"Oh," Gary responded, carefully inspecting his shoes. His hands looked like they itched for something to do. He turned back to the business of sorting through the boxes, looking for whatever he'd been looking for. "Why's that," he said over his shoulder, striving for a casual tone.

"I remembered something today," Cass continued. "I remembered something that, until today, I didn't remember at all. The memory was blazingly vivid. And, like a lot of things in our family, it was both perfectly normal and very weird."

Gary was having a hard time focusing. He pulled a random box out of the middle of a stack and this sent two more tumbling into him.

Cass almost laughed, but swallowed the giggle that threatened to sneak out. "You *sure* I can't help you, Dad?" she asked.

"No, no. Go on, sweetie. You were remembering something?" He pulled his leg free from the box that had pinned him.

"We were in Japan, I think. I was maybe seven years old. You and me and Mom. We were at a cherry blossom festival. The whole grove of trees had exploded in white and pink flowers. It was a beautiful day. And we were all just . . . happy."

Cass scuffed the toe of her sneaker against the cement floor of the garage, staring at the ground. Her father had gone very still. He was looking right at her. She met his eyes.

"Is that a real memory, Dad? Do you remember this?"

He held her eyes.

"Yes, Cassandra. That is a true memory. We traveled to Japan to visit family, as we often did in those days."

He paused, revisiting the scene in his own mind's eye. "And you're right. We were . . . very happy."

He broke eye contact and went back to his boxes, shifting one out of the way and stumbling over another.

"I also remembered something else about that trip," Cass said. "It wasn't just the three of us. There was someone else there."

Cass saw him stiffen for a moment, then continue with the boxes.

"There was an older woman. Tiny. White hair in a bun. Dressed in something like a kimono."

Gary stopped what he was doing. He stood up straight and stretched, his hands in the small of his aching back. He sighed deeply and looked back in Cass's direction, a hint of fear in his eyes.

"Cassandra," he said slowly and sternly, "listen carefully. You are wrong about that part. No one else was there. There was no tiny woman with white hair. You are, I'm afraid, remembering wrong."

Cass felt hurt. And she knew he was lying.

Her weak, wandering eye twitched into focus, a soft burn igniting at the base of the socket, and she felt like she could see right through him. He was afraid. He was trying to protect her. But he was wrong. She didn't need to be protected right now. She needed the truth.

She was the Seer and she needed to *see*.

She felt both angry and sad at the same time. She swallowed hard. "Okay, Dad," she said coldly and shivered again. "I'd better be getting home. Good to see you though."

Her father didn't immediately respond. Cass turned to go. She started down the driveway. She could hear her father tearing tape from the top of a box, rummaging through its contents, and then adding a quiet, "Ah ha."

He called after her. "Cassandra, wait. Wait just a moment please."

He jogged down the driveway to catch her. He had an old book in hand. It had a pink cover with a small combination lock and faded, handwritten pages.

"I'm sorry," he said, pegging the apology to nothing in particular. "This, though, is for you."

He handed her the book. CASSANDRA JONES was written on the front in a seven year-old's handwriting.

"I've been thinking, all day," he confessed, "about that same trip to Japan. About that same visit to the cherry blossom festival. When I woke up this morning, it was the first idea in my head. I lay in bed for a long time thinking about it."

Cass waited for him to continue.

"What are the odds," he said, "that you'd suddenly remember the same thing? Then I was getting ready for bed tonight, but couldn't stop thinking about your journal from that same trip. So I came out to the garage to look for it."

Cass still remembered the combination. She popped the lock and cracked the diary. The book naturally fell open to a spray of cherry blossoms, pressed for decades between the pages. Next to the blossoms, she found a single Japanese kanji written three times: *kibo*.

Cass felt the void inside of her contract as tears snuck into the corners of her eyes. She pulled her father into a reluctant hug. He hesitated, then gave her a brief, fierce squeeze in return.

Their hug was interrupted by a voice from behind them.

"I'm sorry to interrupt," Miranda said. "I really am. But something has come up. And I need Cass."

7

MIRANDA TORE AROUND a street corner in her Audi, fishtailing for a moment onto the far side of the road. Cass braced herself, holding on to the door handle with both hands and wedging her feet into opposite corners under the dash. As a reward for her efforts, she only slid a couple of inches across her leather seat.

Miranda was still wearing her sunglasses even though it was close to midnight now.

Much as I love her, it's a miracle she hasn't killed anyone yet, Cass thought.

It wasn't clear why they were driving this way. They weren't even in any real hurry. They had an appointment—maybe. But even that seemed loosely defined.

Miranda had been hearing rumors for weeks now that the Lost had a new leader. The rumors referred to the new leader as "the Heretic." Her sources couldn't confirm who the Heretic was, but she had her own set of suspicions. Without more information, though, she was *not* yet willing to share those suspicions with her bosses. She would have to go it alone and do some digging first.

Miranda explained that she'd had to do that more and more often recently. In fact, her entire escapade a few months back with Cass, Zach, and Richard was an off-the-books, unauthorized adventure. But once Judas was dead, she couldn't avoid reporting the whole affair. And the powers-that-be were not pleased. They didn't trust Richard York in the first place and they hated, above all, the change and instability that followed Judas's death. She needed more information first. *Then* she could decide what to do, how much to share, and who to trust.

For the moment, though, she only trusted Cass.

"I've got a lead," Miranda said, slamming on the brakes for a stop sign. Cass considered this a good sign —sometimes Miranda treated stop signs as optional. "I've got a lead on a source that might be able to tell us where the Lost are congregating now that Judas's castle has been destroyed."

"Sounds solid," Cass deadpanned. "A lead on a source who might meet us and who might have information about a location where we might be able to find people with more information that we could eventually use to figure out who is leading the Lost now."

"Exactly. You've got it. I'm glad you understand how this works. You're really learning fast." Miranda deadpanned in return, stepping on the gas and looking straight at Cass for a beat longer than felt safe given their rate of acceleration.

They drove for another fifteen minutes, through an industrial park, past the outskirts of town, and pulled up quietly around the side of an abandoned warehouse just off a thickly wooded tree line. They parked in the shadows. If Cass had been assigned to scout a location for a movie where the hero had to meet an informant, this was exactly the kind of place she would have picked.

"Okay," Cass said, craning her neck and looking around the deserted lot, "where are we supposed to meet—"

Miranda cut her off.

"Shhhh," Miranda whispered. "Be quiet. Just listen for a minute and tell me if you hear anything."

They sat in the car in silence, listening. The only sound was the car's overworked engine cooling. Cass was beginning to get the feeling that their possible "source" might not be a friendly (or even willing) participant in tonight's information exchange. Miranda looked steeled for . . . a variety of eventualities.

The trees swayed in the cold wind. An owl hooted. The waning moon shone weakly in the clear night sky.

"Oh, I also brought you something," Miranda said, reaching into the backseat. She pulled out Cass's sword, the one that her mother had left her and that now had a fragment of the One True Cross embedded in its hilt.

Cass accepted the sword but gave Miranda a hard look in return.

"Just in case," Miranda said, "things get a little off-script."

"Right. Just in case," Cass replied, hefting the sword, wondering what she'd gotten herself into.

They could see several pairs of headlights coming down the service road now. Two vans, a black SUV, and a black sedan. They stopped in front of the building. A handful of burly looking guys in leather jackets jumped out and stationed themselves in various, watchful positions near the entrance to the warehouse. One of them undid the heavy padlock, unthreaded chains that secured the main door, and rolled the door back. Both vans and the sedan pulled inside the warehouse.

Cass could tell from their standard issue leather jackets that the crew were Lost.

"I don't like this, Miranda," Cass said. "I don't like the look of it one bit. And there are definitely more of them than there are of us. And why do they always wear those clichéd leather jackets? Is there a vampire dress code? School uniforms?"

"We're just going to take a quick look around," Miranda said, ignoring her snark. "We just need a peek at who's in the backseat of that black sedan."

Miranda cracked her knuckles and rolled her neck, loosening her shoulders. Her eyes glinted green in the moonlight.

"Stay close," Miranda cautioned. She was out her door before Cass knew it and Cass had to hurry to catch up.

They circled around the back of the warehouse, moving silently and staying out of sight. Cass slung her sword across her back, leaving it in its sheath for now. A guard, already bored with guard duty, was positioned at the far corner. They watched him fidget for a moment, shifting from foot to foot, until he couldn't resist the urge to pull out his phone.

Miranda signaled for Cass to take him out. Then, for good measure, emphasized that this needed to be "quiet" by mouthing the word and putting her finger to Cass's lips.

Cass rolled her eyes and batted the finger away.

She crept up behind the man in his tight vampire jeans and heavy vampire boots and leather vampire jacket with chains. She could see, over his shoulder, that he was scrolling through his Instagram feed. LittleBaker53. Cass couldn't help but see what he was looking at. He paused to admire a mouth-watering image of a luscious piece of chocolate cake displayed on an antique yellow plate and beautifully framed by the setting sun.

Cass wondered what filters the photographer had used to create that effect. Then she suddenly realized that she was very hungry again—dinner had never really happened—and her stomach growled with an easily audible rumble.

The guard dropped his phone and reached for his weapon. But before he could reach it, Cass swept his leg, unsheathed her sword, and clocked him on the head with its hilt, all in one smooth motion.

He dropped like a sack of potatoes.

Miranda waved her hands in exasperation, as if to say: stop playing around up there. Cass just pointed to the guy on the ground, patted her belly, and shrugged.

They found a side door and both peeked through its window to get a glance at how the warehouse was laid out on the inside. They couldn't see much, though. Stacks of abandoned crates and boxes crowded near the door obstructed any clear view of the rest of the room.

Miranda closed her eyes, focused her attention, and steepled her index fingers. A spark of green light flickered at their tips. She pinched the light between both thumbs and index fingers and slowly pulled them apart until, in the arc of light between them, a skeleton key materialized. Miranda slid the key into the door's lock, turned the tumblers, and silently opened the door, holding it politely open for Cass.

"Neat trick," Cass couldn't help but whisper even as she wondered why, if Miranda could do tricks like that on command, Cass was the one going through the door first.

From their new vantage point behind the crates and boxes, they could safely take stock of the room. The two vans were parked in the center, flanked by the black sedan. Cass couldn't quite tell what they had in hand, but they were transferring long, heavy bags from one van to the other. Then, with a jolt, she knew exactly what was in them: those long, black bags were body bags. A cold shiver ran down her spine and she gripped her sword more tightly. Miranda squeezed her shoulder reassuringly and moved closer for a better look.

As Miranda moved closer, an enormous man heaved his bulk out of the backseat of the sedan. He made the sedan look like a clown car. When he stood up to his full height, his ponytail swaying, Cass wasn't sure how he'd squeezed into that backseat in the first place. His movements, though, were compact and graceful. He radiated a kind of benevolent competence that seemed at odds with the kind of frantic, agitated hunger that, in Cass's experience, always itched beneath the surface of the Lost.

"Damn," Miranda whispered when she saw him. Cass looked from Miranda back to this giant and felt her stomach clench into a tight little ball: he was looking right at them.

"Hello, Miranda," he said and, with a pair of curt signals, he sent men to flank them from both directions. They wore gas masks and were armed with rifles. At the same moment, the side door behind them banged open and someone tossed a canister of tear gas in their direction.

The smoke spread quickly. Cass's eyes blurred with tears and she doubled over, coughing.

"Cass!" Miranda called.

Cass couldn't catch her breath enough to reply. She could hear that they were already on top of Miranda and that Miranda wasn't going down without a fight. Crates and boxes flew as men in leather jackets and gas masks were tossed aside by an expanding burst of green light. Cass was also pushed back by the force of the blast. She was knocked off her feet and skidded across the warehouse's rough cement floor. The good news, though, was that, for the price of a few bruises, Cass was largely pushed clear of the cloud of tear gas.

She wiped the tears from her eyes, drew in a deep, lung-clearing breath, and tried to zero in on Miranda's location. Through all the smoke, she couldn't see clearly what was happening on the other side of the room. Still, despite the smoke, she didn't have any trouble pin-pointing where all the shouts and screams were coming from.

Cass rolled to her feet and gathered herself to spring in Miranda's direction. But when she took off running, she didn't go anywhere. Like Wile E. Coyote off the edge of a cliff, her legs spun tractionless in midair. Surprised, she craned her neck to see what was happening and found that the monster of a man from the clown car had her hooked by the collar of her jacket. He held her suspended a few feet off the ground. He batted the sword from her hand and it went spinning across the room. He looked slightly amused by the surprised expression on her face and, generally, unconcerned.

Cass tried to kick free, but her legs weren't long enough. The man just extended his arm and held her clear of his torso.

Cass was starting to get pissed. She could hear what a wild scrum Miranda was in. Cass twisted in his grasp, frantic to break free, but didn't go anywhere.

For his part, the man held her up to catch the light from the sedan's headlights, like he was simply curious about something he'd found lying on the ground and was trying to figure out what it was.

"You," he said with a rumbling voice, "are Cassandra Jones?"

Cass couldn't tell from his tone of voice if he'd meant that as a statement or a question—though by the time he'd gotten to the end of the sentence he seemed puzzled enough by what he was seeing that it ended like a question.

He hefted her once or twice, as if trying to find some additional substance to her small, slight frame.

"Cassandra Jones?" he repeated when she didn't reply.

And then it hit Cass: *Yes, damn it, I* am *Cassandra Jones!* When she thought it, she felt the force of it. And, more, when she thought it, she felt the *truth* of it.

Her weak eye burned in her skull. Wisps of white smoke trailed from the corner of her eye and time went slack. Where, a moment before, she'd felt cramped by the inexorable, inevitable crush of time, now it felt like there was room to move, like time had opened out onto a third dimension where the normal rules didn't apply. Here, she could act with a simplicity and clarity of intention that normally escaped her.

"Yes," she calmly said, "I'm Cassandra Jones. Nice to meet you . . . dickhead." She kicked her legs up and locked them around his ham hock of an upper arm, slipped her arms free of the jacket he was holding, and swung to the floor where—mostly because it was the only part of him she could really reach—she used the whole of her momentum to punch him straight in the groin. He wobbled for a moment and then crumpled to his knees, his look of surprise now level with her own look of determination.

Cass spit in his face, but didn't wait around to see what was going to happen next. She didn't think that would hold him long. She darted into the smoke after Miranda.

But she was too late. Through the fog, Cass could make out how the Lost had corralled Miranda with four or five separate ropes and were working in concert now to pin her arms and wrap her up.

"No!" Cass shouted. "Miranda!"

Cass felt a surge of desperation battering the heavy doors in her heart, threatening to break free and sweep her away with them.

Miranda looked up and locked eyes with Cass.

"Cass," she yelled, "these people are not—"

But she was cut off as the men gagged her, bundled her into an open van, and slammed the door shut behind them.

Cass caught the glint of her dropped sword in their headlights and dove for it. As the van sped by, tires smoking, she rammed her sword into the wall of the van and held on for dear life as it accelerated toward the door. The driver, surprised, spotted her in his side view mirror, hanging from the side of the van. At the last moment, as they cleared the door, he jerked the van toward the wall in an effort to scrape her off. The wall clipped Cass on the shoulder and side of her head.

Cass rolled like a rag doll across the pavement, her sword clattering next to her. Her vision swam in and out of focus as the van's taillights receded down the drive. But, despite her blurry vision, she didn't have any trouble recognizing her old friend, the giant, when he stepped into view.

"It was nice to meet you Cassandra Jones," he said, his voice slightly higher now than it had been before.

Cass reached weakly for her sword.

"Good night, now" he said, as his huge hand reached out toward her, swallowing her entire face, and everything went black.

8

IT WAS EARLY. Miranda's Audi was parked crooked in the street in front of Zach's apartment. It was the only place Cass could think to go.

She dragged herself to the door, her shoulder bruised and her forehead bloody, and gave it a half-hearted knock.

Nothing.

She tried again, leaning her head against the door and pounding with both fists. When Zach pulled the door open, rubbing sleep from his eyes and dressed only in boxers, Cass saw that she'd left a bloody mark on the wood.

"Sorry," she said, waving at the mark and tipping forward through the door.

With her arm slung around his neck, Zach helped her inside.

The apartment was gorgeous. It was all clean lines, open spaces, modern furniture, and high end appliances. Everything was spotless and in its place. A couple of striking, original pieces of art were lit up on the wall by recessed lighting. An entire wall was nothing but built-in bookshelves. The books may even have been color-coded. And, as far as she could tell, Zach didn't own a TV.

Cass had often dropped Zach off at his apartment after work, but she'd never accepted his invitations to come in. It had seemed like a line she shouldn't cross. She valued his friendship too much. She didn't know what she'd expected, but it wasn't this. This was no barista's apartment. This was not the life of a self-taught college drop-out getting by on minimum wage.

Before she had a chance to comment, her knees went weak and Zach helped her into a chair.

"Cass," he said, eyeing the blood on her head, his voice thick with concern. "What happened?"

She took a deep breath. Once she started, everything poured out all at once.

"They've got Miranda. There was a giant man in an abandoned warehouse. I punched him in the balls. The Lost have her. Miranda was tracking down a lead on who their new leader is. She took me along for backup. There was tear gas. It was a trap. Miranda almost killed us driving over there. She's such a terrible driver. I attacked a van with my sword but when I had to fight the wall, the wall won and they got away. That's how I hurt myself."

Zach sat perched on the arm of the sofa next to her, trying to take it all in. He reached out several times to check her head wound, but Cass waved him off.

Cass couldn't quite decide what to make of Zach's expression. It was two parts concerned and two parts unreadable. But the thought of Miranda at mercy of those vampires solicited a wave of anger that nudged her back toward coherence.

Cass heaved herself out of the armchair and, in the process, knocked the throw pillow to the floor. Zach scooped up the pillow and returned it to its proper spot. She took a couple of unsteady steps toward the kitchen, stopped and looked at her own reflection in the polished stainless steel of the refrigerator, and groaned at the site of the blood. Though her shoulder would be sore for a couple of days, the head wound was, fortunately, superficial.

Cass turned on the water in the sink, took a long drink from the tap, and washed her face. She saw Zach wince when she reached for the white, neatly folded dishtowel and held it to her bloody forehead—but he bit his tongue and didn't say anything.

"We have to go after her, Zach," Cass said quietly.

Cass opened the freezer, popped out a couple of ice cubes, wrapped them in her bloody towel, and pressed them gingerly to her face.

"Cass," Zach tried again, softly shaking his head. "I think this may be out of our league."

"You're not hearing me, Zach," Cass continued. "We don't have a choice. If we don't go after her, nobody will. She's my aunt. My family. And, apart from my dad, she's all I've got left. I'm not just going to sit on my hands and hope for the best."

Zach nodded his head in reluctant agreement. He might be willing to pass the buck when it came to Miranda, but he couldn't resist that kind of plea from Cass.

Cass could see that she had him. A tiny smile shone through the worry on her face.

"Thank you, Zach," she said. "Seriously. I wouldn't even know where to begin without your help." She removed the bloody wad of ice from her forehead. Her hair was matted, her lip was split, and she had dark circles under eyes.

"I could kiss you for this," she teased. She felt the beginning tendrils of guilt start to grow in her gut as Richard's face flashed across her mind, but she quickly pushed them back down. That wasn't going to help anyone.

Zach involuntarily blushed as Cass, not quite as playfully as she'd intended, admired him in the flattering cut of his boxers.

"Uhhh, right," Zach said, retreating to grab a pair of pants from his bedroom. "Maybe later."

When he returned, he not only had pants but some antibacterial ointment and butterfly bandages.

"Sit down, Beautiful," he said.

She gratefully took a seat at the kitchen counter and, this time, let him clean and bandage the wound. He brushed her hair back from her face and lifted her chin to get a better look at the cut. Cass was careful to avoid his eyes until he was done.

He tossed the packaging and bloody towel into the garbage can.

"Okay," he said, sizing her up. "That's better. I'll take that kiss now."

Cass smiled, tilted her head, puckered up, and closed her eyes.

Zach kissed the wound he'd just bandaged and said, "Also, I've got an idea about where we might start. There's a guy I've been hearing about recently, an information broker, that we could go see."

"Sounds good," Cass said. "When do we start?"

"We can start," Zach replied, "as soon as we finally have a serious conversation about your couch."

9

CASS'S APARTMENT WAS a comparative wreck. This was especially true of the old couch with its cracked leather cushions.

It was mid-morning by the time they made it back over there. Zach had a grabbed a duffle bag of gear from his own apartment, but he'd also insisted that, wherever their search for Miranda took them, that search would have to begin at Cass's apartment. And it would have to begin *after* Cass had a chance to rest.

Cass was so tired and wrung out from the past twenty-four hours—the dreams, the sparring, the memory, the visit to her dad, the fight at the warehouse, the loss of Miranda—that she couldn't even think of decent arguments against this plan. At this point, coffee alone wasn't going to pull her through.

First thing, Zach ushered Cass into the bathroom, set the hot water running for her shower, and then firmly shut the door behind him. While Cass was showering, he called in sick to Java's palace. Avoiding the couch, he parked himself on a hard kitchen chair and sorted through his gear, trying to decide what they'd need for something like this. He decided to go for warm layers, well-worn boots, and a warm but light nylon jacket. Long before Cass exited the shower, he'd stripped down to his boxers and re-dressed as some version of tactical-Zach, stuffing various pockets full of small but useful items they might need.

Except for the dark circles under her eyes, Cass almost looked like herself when she emerged from the bathroom in a towel and a puff of steam. Zach handed her the similarly dark, layered clothes he'd picked out for her from her closet and sent her back in again.

Cass reappeared in a couple of minutes. "Okay," Cass said, cinching her belt. "Let's go then."

"Sure," Zach countered. "Just one last thing: you've got to close your eyes for thirty minutes and get some rest."

"Zaaaccchh," Cass resisted, her voice trailing off in exasperation, "we've got to go. We've got to find Miranda."

"Yes," Zach agreed, "but you've also got to be worth something when we get there. Otherwise, we'll just get eaten or, you know, become vampires ourselves. Both of which are bad."

He eyed the bed in the corner of the room and opted for the couch instead. He sat down and patted the spot next to him. "Just thirty minutes. Sit down here with me and close your eyes for half an hour and then we'll go."

"Fine," Cass said, tired of arguing. She plopped down on the couch and curled up next to him, her head resting on his shoulder.

"Good. Now close your eyes."

"Okay, but I'm not going to sleep. I'm way too wired to sleep. In fact, I've barely slept for months."

She snuggled closer, closed her eyes, and tried to find somewhere more comfortable to lay her head than his bony shoulder. Gravity decided for her. Her eyes fluttered shut and she was basically snoring before her head hit his lap. Zach pulled a blanket from the back of the couch and draped it over her. He smoothed her still damp hair, squeezed her shoulder, and bent to give her a peck on the cheek. As he leaned in, Cass murmured something in her sleep, turned toward him, and brushed his lips with a kiss.

Cass slept for more than twelve hours. It was ten at night when, finally, she stretched and opened her eyes. Zach was seated at the kitchen table with his laptop. A ping indicated that he'd been messaging someone. The only light in the room came from the street and the glow of his screen. Cass sat up, tossed the blanket onto the back of the couch, and pulled her hair back into a ponytail. Zach leaned back in his chair and flipped on the kitchen lights.

"You look human again," Zach said.

"I *feel* human again," Cass said, echoing his judgment.

Her head felt clear—the white, chaotic noise that had clouded her mind for weeks had receded. She rolled her shoulder in its socket with only a hint of soreness. She couldn't even be upset that he'd let her sleep so long, not when the results were so clearly what she needed. *If we'd left from Zach's apartment, I was so far gone I'd be dead by now,* Cass realized. *The first vampire we saw would have kicked my butt.*

"Dr. Riviera, you're hired," Cass exclaimed.

"Excellent. My next prescription is for actual food. Sit down." He plated a giant omelet for her and added a tall glass of orange juice. When he pulled the juice out of the fridge, she saw that he'd restocked it while she was passed out on the couch. Also, the apartment was, in general, suspiciously clean and tidy.

Cass was ravenous. She shoveled it down. The more embarrassed she felt by her manners, the more Zach seemed to enjoy watching her eat. She sat back, patted her flat stomach, and tried, for Zach's sake, to manage something like a burp. He was impressed.

"It turns out," Cass said, "that all I really need to get along in life is someone to cook for me, clean my apartment, and tuck me into bed. All I really needed was"— Cass almost said "a mother" but instead, after a moment's hesitation, said—"a wife."

Zach laughed as he refolded her blanket and laid it neatly over the back of the couch.

Cass pulled on her socks and boots.

"Now," she said, "let's find Miranda."

He gathered her dishes, rinsed them in the sink, dried them, and replaced them in the cupboards. He glanced at Cass and the couch over his shoulder.

"First, the couch," Zach replied. Cass started to shake her head vehemently, but Zach insisted. "It's important. I promise." Cass stared at him.

"Let's start with this," he said. "You tell me about the couch." He looked so serious, eyes wide and pleading. She gave in.

"We've had it for years," Cass started. "It's been around longer than me. It's been around longer than my dad. It was my mom's in college. It feels like part of the family. Dad was happy, though, to send it with me when I asked if I could take it to my own place. Umm, what else? It's very comfortable. But . . . it's also weird. Like, sometimes it seems to move around the room on its own—a couple feet in one direction, or a couple feet in another. And sometimes I find things in it that I have no idea how they got there. Money, books, underwear, silverware, you name it."

Cass fell silent for a moment. Zach waited for her to go on.

"And sometimes," she continued, "I get this really weird feeling like . . . like there's nothing inside the couch. Like, literally *nothing* is inside the couch. A void. Like, if I pulled off the cushions I wouldn't see the couch frame or the floor but just some kind of hungry, yawning abyss."

She stopped herself, wondering how crazy she sounded. *It's a couch, dammit*, she thought to herself, *not an existential crisis!*

Zach just nodded his head in agreement. Then, to her surprise, he said: "It seems like you basically already know what there is to know about your couch. You've just never taken it seriously. In a nutshell, the truth is that your couch is a kind of door. It's a kind of 'portal' to a part of the world where magic and vampires and such are taken for granted as part of the fabric of reality."

Cass stared at him, her mouth slack.

"Grab your gear," he said. "I thought you were in a hurry. It's time to go."

Well, what did you expect? she asked herself. *It's no weirder than vampires who only wear black leather being a real thing.*

Cass grabbed her jacket and sword. Zach shrugged into his own jacket, pulled a cushion off the couch, and set it carefully to one side. Even from a few feet away, Cass could see that, inside of the couch, a narrow set of stairs descended steeply into darkness.

"Cassandra Jones," Zach said, stepping into the couch, "welcome to the Underside."

10

THE WALLS OF the tight stairwell were cold and smooth. Cass trailed her fingers along the side of the wall as she descended but, in the darkness, she couldn't quite tell what they were made of—concrete? stone? The stairwell emptied into a long, narrow hallway. In the middle distance, a bare bulb hung from the ceiling and burned with a green tinged light.

Zach looked back to make sure that Cass had followed him down. She was right on his heels. She felt a little queasy, like her normal relationship to gravity had been tweaked somehow, but nodded for him to go on.

Zach pressed down the hallway, Cass in tow. He seemed to know where they were going. About halfway down the hallway, adjacent to the hanging bulb, they passed a heavy, unmarked door.

Cass felt the door tug at her, call for her, and stopped. The door was flush with the wall. It had a lock for a key but no external handle. Cass grazed the lock with her thumb—it was extremely cold—then traced the edges of the door, from top to bottom, with her fingertips.

"Zach, what is this door?" she asked.

Zach turned back. He hadn't realized Cass had stopped. He examined the door. He hadn't seen it as he'd hurried past.

"To be honest," he said, "I don't know. I've never seen a door like this in the Underside before. There are stairwells and hallways and huge hubs—but not doors like this."

Cass pressed her ear against the door, but didn't hear anything.

"We'd better go, though," Zach prompted. "Now that we're ready, it's important to move as quickly as we can."

Cass agreed and they continued at a brisk pace down the hall, hit a ninety-degree turn when the hallway forked, and then continued down another hallway that looked basically identical to the first.

"The basics of this place—of the Underside—are pretty straightforward," Zach explained. "We don't know who originally built it or discovered it, or how long it's been around, but these days it basically gives those who don't quite fit in with the everyday world a place to call home. Magicians, the Lost, the Turned," he paused and looked back at her, adding, "Seers."

Their hallway come to another "T" and, after a glance in both directions, Zach choose left.

"The Underside," he continued, "is like a fourth spatial dimension appended to the everyday world. It doesn't belong to that world and it isn't constrained by the same rules or the normal laws of physics. The Underside does, though, at certain key locations, crossover with the everyday world."

Zach reached back and took her hand, flashed her a crooked smiled, and they broke into a light jog. The end of their current hallway opened onto an array of bright lights.

"Sometimes, these crossover sites just amount to small portals like the one we used in your couch. Usually, portals like that have to be specially constructed. But, for the most part, these crossover sites mark places where the Underside pokes out into the Overside and occupies shared space with the ordinary world. There are a dozen such overlapping sites across the planet. These sites functions as 'hubs,' as small cities in their own right that are hidden behind the ordinary facades visible from the Overside."

Zach gave her hand a squeeze.

"Hubs," he said, "like this."

They emerged all at once from their narrow hallway into an enormous domed space, filled with a twilight sky and the busy lights and sounds of a small city.

Cass's jaw dropped, her mouth forming an involuntary "O." They'd emerged in an alleyway. Cass took a couple of steps into the street and spun in a slow circle, head craned back, trying to take it in.

"Okay," she said, trying to process this, "okay. Before I get too far in redrawing my internal map of the world, are there any other hidden planets or alternate dimensions I should know about?"

"This is the only other one you need to know about . . . for now," Zach said, winking.

Cass punched him in the shoulder.

"Owww," he groused, rubbing the bruise.

"What else do I need to know, then, about this one?"

Zach picked up the thread of his explanation, keeping Cass at arm's length in case she took another swing at him.

"Like I was saying before I was interrupted, the Underside isn't constrained by all the normal laws of physics. For instance, the buildings that occupy crossover sites are much larger on the inside than on the outside. Entire Underside cities like this one unfold inside of what, from the Overside, look like normal office buildings or casinos or monasteries or whatever. Also, hubs often have allegiances and this particular hub is mostly aligned with the Turned."

They worked their way out from the edges of the dome and into a main thoroughfare. The street was packed with people and vendors. There were a couple of rickshaws, but no cars. Most buildings were two or three stories tall, but a handful of buildings in the center were glass and steel office towers. In general, the place had the feel of a festive, cosmopolitan bazaar.

"There are two other things you should know," Zach said. He slipped an arm around her shoulder, pulling her closer so that they wouldn't get separated as they weaved through the crush. "The first is that, though these crossover sites are spread out across the world, the distances between them are walkable. We just left your apartment in Oregon and walked for fifteen minutes. But this hub, the hub we're in now, overlaps with the Overside in London. If we stepped outside, we could have lunch in Hyde Park."

Crap, Cass thought. *I should have brought my passport.*

"The second thing to know," Zach continued, "is that the unusual powers manifest in the Overside by practitioners of magic—or vampires or seers—are grounded in and amplified by the weird rules that govern the Underside."

They stopped in front of what looked like a bar or strip club. A neon sign outlining the figure of a woman blinked and beckoned over the entrance. Next to the image, a scrawl of neon tubes spelled out "BOOBS"—but a section of the lights had burned out years ago so that, now, the sign just read "BO-BS."

"There's something about the Underside," Zach concluded, "that is open to manipulation by mind. In the Overside, I can *know* the everyday world with my mind. But in the Underside, I can *change* the world with my mind. In the end, understanding your own powers will depend on understanding how they're grounded in the weird rules of this part of the world."

His voice trailed off. He saw Cass staring up skeptically at the sign.

"That's all we've got time for now," he said. "Stay close. And welcome to Bob's."

He pulled the door open and held it for her. Cass crossed her arms defensively across her chest and stepped inside.

The lights were dim and music blared. Cass had no idea what time of day it was in the Underside, but business was brisk. Most of it centered around the bar, but parts of it were clustered around the platforms, scattered around the room, that displayed the house dancers.

Surveying the space, Cass noticed that every one of the dancers was a man in his early twenties, dressed in nothing but a thong. This tuned her in to the fact that practically everyone else in the bar was a woman.

Whatever this place used to be, she thought to herself, watching the dancers bob and gyrate, *it doesn't look like an accident that it's now called Bo-bs instead of Boobs.*

Zach was at her elbow. He seemed a little surprised himself.

"Not what you remember?" Cass asked, giving him a pinch.

"Uhhh, not exactly." Zach said. "But it's been awhile."

He pointed across the crowded space toward a service door, and added, "We need to get to that door on the far side of the room. That's where we'll find the guy we're looking for."

Cass nodded. They plunged into the crowd and headed toward the door.

It didn't take long, though, before Zach started drawing a lot of attention. The mood in the room was boisterous and loose. The party had been going for a while, a lot of alcohol had been consumed, and Zach stood out in the press of laughing and dancing women.

Whistles and cat calls started to follow them. Hands reached out to snag him. About halfway across the room, Zach got pinned against a post by woman with pink hair and black fingernails who growled at him playfully, snuggled up close, and slipped a hand up under his t-shirt to stuff a twenty dollar bill into the waistline of his jeans.

"Whoa, whoa, whoa ladies," Zach said, his hands up. "Just passing through here. Not part of the show."

But this mild protest just set up a howl of laughter from the knot of women who'd closed in around them. A dozen hands were raised in the air, waving twenties, trying to squeeze closer.

Oh hell, Cass thought, *you're too damn cute for your own good, Zach.*

"Ladies!" Cass yelled, raising her sword in the air, trumping their twenties. "That's all for now—he's with me!"

Everyone stopped and turned to see what was happening. The music stopped and everyone went silent.

Cass grabbed a fistful of Zach's t-shirt.

"He's mine," she said, mustering a stern note of authority to go with her sword. "Now go find your own."

When the ladies got a look at Cass with her sword, her fistful of Zach's t-shirt, and the pissed look on her face, the energy went out of the crowd. A chorus of boos went up. Then the music started up again and everyone went back to what they'd been doing before.

Cass hauled Zach the rest of the way across the room by her fistful of shirt and didn't let go until they were almost to the door.

"We're barely down here five minutes and, already, I had to rescue your ass," Cass quipped. "What kind of tour guide are you?"

"Cass," Zach said, half joking, half serious, "you're my hero."

He fished the twenty out of his pants and offered it to her. Cass swiped it out of his hand and stuffed it into her own pocket.

"Alright. Enough with the gratitude and puppy dog eyes," Cass ordered. "Let's do what we came to do and get out of here."

The door they'd been aiming for was guarded by a bouncer, a towering woman—Cass was pretty sure it was a woman—in a black leather vest, heavy eye shadow, and tight jeans that said: "if you think I'm a vampire, you're probably right."

Zach offered the bouncer his winningest smile. "We're here to see Amare," he said. Then, in response to the bouncer's blank stare, added, "It's urgent."

This almost made the bouncer smile.

"What's the password?" she asked.

"Ummm, the password," Zach stalled. "The password is, uhhhh . . ."

"Wrong answer," the bouncer said as she grabbed Zach by the throat and lifted him off his feet.

11

ZACH'S FACE TURNED purple then blue. The tips of his toes scraped the ground but didn't offer any traction. He tried to pry the bouncer's hands away, but her grip was too strong.

He choked out a couple of unlikely passwords: "Open sesame . . . abracadabra . . . rook to knight one . . . please?"

This just made the bouncer more angry and she shook him like a doll.

Cass unsheathed her sword again and, with two quick strokes, gave the bouncer a haircut on one side and a wicked scratch, welling with blood, on the other cheek. It might have just been the lighting, but the sword glowed with a faint, white light. Cass held the point of the blade to the bouncer's throat.

"This is our password," she said.

The bouncer dropped Zach and stepped back in awe. She could sense that the sword, apart from whatever else it was, contained a powerful relic—a fragment of the One True Cross.

"Correct," she said, wiping blood from her cheek with the back of her hand. "That's a bona fide password. Let me tell him you're here."

The bouncer slipped inside the door and then returned a moment later.

"Amare will see you now," she said, ushering them inside the backroom.

Zach, his face still red, risked a wink at the bouncer as he followed Cass inside. She curled a lip at him and he hurried through the door. Still looking over his shoulder, he bumped into Cass who'd stopped just inside the door. Whatever they'd expected to find inside, it wasn't this.

The room was large. Near the center of the room, Amare was seated at a desk. A handful of associates were positioned around the room. An antique, rotary telephone was attached to the wall behind him. The rest of the room was filled with a vast, complicated web of pneumatic tubes like the ones that bank tellers use, branching out into various walls, but all leading in the end toward Amare's desk.

Zach took a protective step forward, positioning himself between Cass and Amare—though this seemed ridiculous to Cass given that she'd saved *him* twice in the past five minutes.

Canisters whizzed by through the tubes, landing near Amare's desk with a vacuum-fueled "thunk" of compressed air. The desk was elaborately carved. Amare

appeared to be in his early twenties but his command-
ing presence hinted that Cass shouldn't take that for
granted. He radiated an unusual kind of peace and
confidence. His white shirt contrasted sharply with his
deep black skin and when he issued a couple of com-
mands to his associates, it was obvious that his English
was heavily accented by his native French. Given his
inflections, Cass guessed that he was probably from
North Africa, maybe Morocco.

He was, it seemed clear, an information broker,
stationed at the heart of his pneumatic web like a spider
awaiting its prey.

Zach and Cass waited patiently while he cleared a
few items off his desk. Whatever system of exchange he
was running, Cass couldn't make any sense of it. The
canisters that arrived were filled with nonsensical knick-
knacks like collectible spoons and gift shop shot glasses.
There didn't seem to be any paper involved. The cute
salt shakers and beanie babies that he shoved into canisters and sent back in the other direction didn't seem to
make any more sense than what had arrived. Amare,
though, proceeded as if the symbolic value of all these
exchanges was as obvious and natural as a series of
letters scrawled on a page.

Finally, Amare looked up at them. His gaze was cold
and appraising as he took Zach's measure. But he
couldn't quite conceal a shock of pleasure and recogni-
tion when he realized who Cass was.

"Mr. Riviera," he said. "And Ms. Jones. It's a pleasure to meet you. I'm glad you survived the interview at the door." He glanced at Zach and smiled at Cass.

Zach's face was still a bit red. When Amare mentioned their "interview," he involuntarily rolled his head to the side, cracking his neck and loosening the tight muscles.

"What can I do for you two," Amare asked.

"We need information," Zach said. "I heard that you might be able to help us."

"Both of those things," Amare said in his accented English, "are obviously true. What, specifically, do you need."

"Miranda Byrne. She was abducted last night. We need to know who has her and where."

A canister whizzed by through a tube that ran above Zach's head. Amare chewed on what Zach had said, swapped out a Topps baseball card for a ballpoint pen, and sent the canister back.

When he looked back up, his eyes were hard and narrow. "Yes. I heard," he said. "But I'm afraid that I can't help you with that. It is, shall we say, a bit above *your* pay grade."

"Now wait a minute," Zach started before Amare raised a hand and cut him off.

"Please," Cass interjected, her voice betraying more emotion than she intended. "We've got to find her. You've got to help us."

Amare was taken aback by the raw sincerity of her request. But still, he shook his head.

"You misunderstand," Amare said, "this decision is out of my hands. It is above my pay grade as well. There is nothing I can do for—"

Amare, though, was himself cut off by the phone on the wall behind him. He leaned back in his office chair and lifted the handle from the receiver, unspooling its long, curled cord as he turned back to his desk.

"Yes, ma'am," he said. "I see . . . No, ma'am . . . I will make sure it's done."

He replaced the phone in its cradle.

"It seems you've been given a special dispensation," he said.

Cass smiled hopefully, but Amare raised a finger in warning, stalling her celebration.

"But it's going to cost you," he continued. "I have something that you want. You must, in turn, supply for me something I need."

Cass nodded, eager to agree. Zach held back, his eyes narrowing.

"What do you want?" Zach asked, taking a protective step back in Cass's direction.

"I need a relic," Amare answered. "A powerful relic that is protected by a powerful spell. I need the chains of St Paul. Bring them to me and I'll tell you what you need to know."

Cass knew exactly what he meant. She was familiar with this relic. The chains of St. Paul were on display in a basilica in Rome. They were, according to tradition, the very chains that bound the apostle Paul when he arrived in Rome for his trial in 61 AD. He was found guilty and sentenced to death for being a Christian. The relic wouldn't be hard to find. The trick, evidently, would be acquiring it.

"We'll do it," Cass blurted out before Zach could say anything. "The relic is yours."

"Excellent," Amare said, "excellent. Move, of course, as quickly as you can to acquire it. The chains aren't going anywhere, but my information about Ms. Byrne's whereabouts may certainly prove to be time sensitive."

He gestured to one of his associates as a series of new canisters whizzed through the tubes. "Show them the door," he said.

Cass was ready to go, anxious to get started. Zach was a bit more reluctant to accept that the meeting was actually over. But it didn't matter either way. Amare's associates herded them toward the door.

But as they were being hustled through the door and back into the bar, Amare called out to them.

"Oh," he said, "good luck. And be sure, Ms. Jones, to say hello to your friend, Richard York, for me. We go way back."

Cass's eyes went wide, her mouth hung open.

Say hello to Richard? Richard is dead! And despite herself, she was suddenly back there, watching the stones crash down around them. Every time she lost him, the loss seemed to cut deeper. This was why she needed Zach—he showed up. He was there for her. He was not a loss.

Cass started as she realized the door was closing.

"Stop! No! What!?" Cass cried as she tried to squeeze back inside. But the door had already slammed shut and its bolt had, with a decisive clunk, been slid home.

12

AMARE COULD HEAR that, on the far side of the door, Cass was not going quietly. She pounded the door with her fists, shouting, until the bouncer hauled her away. He had intended to stir the pot by bringing up Richard, but he hadn't intended to solicit that kind of reaction. There was, apparently, more there than he'd thought.

Amare signaled for his associates to turn down the lights, clear the room, and leave him alone. They left through a side door. He leaned back in his chair and stretched. The tubes kept whizzing. He put his head in his hands, his elbows propped on the desk, and gently massaged his temples with his thumbs.

"Why did you add that bit about Richard?" a soft voice asked from deep in the shadows behind him. "It was unnecessary. You hurt her."

Amare wasn't surprised at the voice or the question. He knew she would want to see the wheels of her larger plan finally, after so many years, start turning.

Amare pulled open a desk drawer and extracted a small pocketknife. It was razor sharp. He tested it against the pad of his thumb, drawing a thin line of blood. He sucked the blood clean and began, idly, to add some definition to an unfinished carving in the top of the desk. The whole surface of the desk was tattooed with an elaborate field of interlocking images and words and scrollwork.

"I wanted to see what would happen," he said. "I wanted to read her reaction for myself. And I especially wanted to see if it was true, that she had, in some significant way, allowed herself to love Richard . . . to love a vampire."

"I see," the shadowy voice replied from an entirely different location in the room. "Is that all?"

Amare worked skillfully with the knife. He paused and gently blew the image free of shavings. He looked up, toward the direction from which the voice had last come.

"No," he admitted. "There was something else, too. I wanted, if possible, to plant a wedge between her and the boy. If she grows too attached to Zach, if she comes to trust the Shield too deeply, everything will be harder for us."

"You did well," the voice said from nowhere in particular.

They waited together in silence. The only sound was the knife.

"Master," Amare continued, picking up the thread of his often expressed concern, "it may be a mistake to wait. Perhaps we should act quickly and bring Cass in now."

More silence.

A hooded figure, the Heretic, stepped from the shadows behind Amare and rested its hand lightly on his shoulder.

"You are like a son to me, Amare," the Heretic said. "You are like the son I almost had but never knew. And, right now, I trust you more than anyone else in the world. But it's not time yet. We will need to carefully and patiently prepare her before trying to turn her. We will only get one chance. And if we fail, all is lost."

The Heretic leaned over Amare's shoulder to see what he'd been working on with his knife. Embedded in beautiful scrollwork, he'd carved "LUKE 15:24" into the surface of the desk.

"Be patient, Amare. Be patient. She will come to us. She will learn that not all of the Lost are lost."

13

WITH LITTLE CEREMONY, Cass and Zach were tossed out of BO-BS and back onto the street. It was hard to tell what time it was down here in the Underside—it always seemed to be twilight—but the streets were even busier now than they had been before.

Cass felt both elated and frightened at the idea that Richard might still be alive. Part of her was already convinced that it was true: he was alive. But part of her didn't dare believe it. She was only just barely pulling herself out of that tailspin. And helping Miranda had to take priority over everything else.

She wiped her eyes with the back of her sleeve, surprised to discover that actual tears had welled up.

Zach took her by the arm. They worked their way into the street and surrendered themselves to the flow of the crowd. Cass tried to pull herself together. They'd made a deal: they needed to recover the chains of St. Paul. Then they could track down Miranda. As she tried to focus, though, a black wave of emotion swept over her, fracturing her attention and bringing her to a standstill. Zach stopped too, buffering her from the crowd that flowed around them.

Cass looked up at Zach's face. She used her sleeve to wipe her eyes again. She shook her head and said, "Sorry. It's just . . . Richard."

Zach nodded in agreement. It was obvious, though, that he had not been affected by the news in the same way she had. In fact, he seemed a bit distant, a bit cold to the touch. And more, Cass noted to herself, he didn't seem surprised.

Cass searched Zach's face, looking for an answer to her unspoken question. Zach looked away.

"You knew," she said. "You already knew."

"Cass . . ." he responded, touching her shoulder reassuringly.

But she could read the truth in his eyes. He'd already known that Richard was still alive. An ember of anger flared in her weak eye as she focused her full attention on him.

"Don't you dare lie to me, Zach. I'm the goddam Seer," Cass said, almost spitting her last words, poking a finger into his chest. "How long have you known?"

Zach couldn't meet her eyes. He didn't know what to say.

"How long? Why didn't you tell me?"

"I just wanted to protect you," he finally blurted out, meeting her eyes for just a second before glancing away again. "I was worried about you."

Cass knew that this was true. He wasn't lying about that. But it was also obvious that this was only part of the truth. He was hiding something. There was more to it than his honest desire to protect her.

Another black wave of hopelessness rose in her and crashed against the heavy, but weakening doors in her heart. Her body was rocked from the inside out.

Zach looked at her in alarm as the color drained from her face, her cheeks ashen.

Cass leaned into him. She took another fistful of his shirt, this time in earnest, and halfheartedly pounded her fists against his chest. She pulled his face down toward hers.

"Listen to me, Zach," she said, her voice soft but dark. "If I can't trust you, what have I got left?"

Zach closed his eyes, ashamed, and nodded his head.

Cass let go of his shirt, turned her back, and started to walk away. She let herself be carried along again by the wave of pedestrians.

Zach came to himself and rushed to catch up, calling after her.

"Cass," he shouted. "Cass, wait up. I'm sorry. It wasn't up to me."

The apology hit Cass like a brick. She swiveled on her heels and turned back to him, taking him by surprise.

"You're sorry?" she asked. "You're genuinely sorry? The whole thing was truly out of your hands? It wasn't up to you? You had orders or something to keep it a secret?" She waited a beat, letting her questions sink in. "If that's true, then make it up to me."

Zach gulped, his Adam's apple bobbing, but he steeled himself. It was clear that if he had to choose between whoever was apparently giving him orders and Cass, he was going to choose Cass.

Cass let him have it. "Where is Richard? Do you know how to find him? Don't lie to me."

Zach didn't answer.

Cass thought he might be avoiding the question. But he wasn't. He was looking intently over her shoulder. He was staring at something just behind her, a hint of a smile on his lips.

Almost afraid to check, Cass slowly turned to see what he was staring at. They were standing deep in the shadow of a glass and steel office tower. It soared into the air above them.

A giant corporate logo hung above the main entrance to the building. The sign read: YORK ENTERPRISES.

14

CASS DIDN'T HESITATE. She also didn't wait to see if Zach was coming with her. She headed straight for the front door and into the lobby of the building. Zach scrambled to catch up.

The lobby walls were, on three sides, made entirely of glass and open to the height of four stories. It captured the Underside's perpetual twilight to stunning effect. A handful of expensive couches were artfully arranged in cozy groups around the space. A bank of elevators occupied the far side of the lobby. But a guard desk, a handful of armed men, and a set of metal detectors were positioned between the elevators and the main entrance.

Cass felt a calm settle over her, a sense of clarity and purpose that she'd been missing for months. She pulled her hairband free and let her black hair fall loose to her shoulders. Her eyes were focused. She radiated a subtle white light. She straightened her jacket, smoothed her form-fitting sweater, and strode across the lobby to the guard desk. Every head in the lobby swiveled to watch her.

"Oh, shit," Zach whispered to himself as he finally pushed through the door and caught sight of her.

Cass stopped at the desk. Without missing a beat, she said, "I need to see Richard York."

The guard, gangly in a uniform whose sleeves were too short, stuttered a response.

"Do . . . do you have an appointment . . . ma'am?" he managed.

"No. But tell him that Cassandra Jones is here."

The guard pulled uselessly at the cuff of his shirt, as if to make himself look more presentable or authoritative in the face of Cass's beauty and assertiveness. It didn't work. He hesitated, trying to decide on a response.

But Cass wasn't waiting. The subtle sense that she was radiating light from her own person grew stronger.

"Now," she snapped.

"Yes, ma'am," the guard agreed, picking up his phone's receiver and hastily dialing a number.

Cass watched him carefully while he waited for someone to answer the phone on the other end. Finally someone answered. Cass couldn't tell what they were saying but the woman's voice on the other end sounded clipped and annoyed. The guard seemed almost as nervous to speak with her as he was to deal with Cass.

He relayed Cass's request and then visibly cringed at the response, holding the receiver out and away from his ear, as if it could hurt him.

"Yes, Ms. Krishnamurti. Sorry to bother you, ma'am. Yes, ma'am. I'll let her know." He finished the call and slowly returned the receiver to its cradle, reluctant to turn and face Cass with bad news.

"I'm sorry to say, ma'am, that Mr. York is not here today. Perhaps if you contacted his office and arranged an appointment—"

Cass looked him in the eye.

"You're lying," she said simply as she swung herself gracefully over the countertop, twisted the guard's arm behind his back, and gently planted his face on the counter next to the phone.

It happened so fast the guard didn't have time to react.

"I'm afraid I'll need to borrow your key," Cass said. "I hope this doesn't get you into too much trouble."

He grimaced at the thought of what the woman on the other end of the phone would do to him if he didn't stop Cass and, in response, Cass put a little extra pressure on his twisted arm. His face went red. While he squirmed, she smoothly unclipped the key card from his belt and took a step back.

As soon as she let go, the guard spun and took a swing at her. Cass stepped under his extended arm, hooked his foot, sat him down in his wheeled office chair, and, with a little shove, sent him rolling across the polished marble floor.

"I was telling the truth," she said to no one in particular. "I *need* to see him."

The handful of remaining guards had a more serious look—for one, their uniforms appeared to fit. They pulled billy clubs and Tasers and zeroed in on her.

Cass didn't pay them any attention. She headed for the bank of elevators with her newly acquired key card. White light wafted like steam from the back of her jacket.

For Cass, time went slack and the world around her felt like it had slowed to a crawl.

One guard approached from the left and another from the right. Cass kept walking. When the first one got close enough to swing his billy club at her head, she took a half-step to the side, tripped him, and sent him crashing into the second guard whose Taser was already crackling and ready. The first guard's billy club connected squarely with the second guard's head while the second guard's Taser connected squarely with the first man's armpit. Together, they slumped to the ground in a heap. They looked to be resting peacefully in each other's arms.

Of the two remaining guards, one charged, aiming to tackle Cass. Cass waited until the last moment, vaulted over his back, and sent him crashing into a potted plant.

Cass looked the last guard in the eye and shrugged at him, as if to suggest that none of this was really her fault. He took a look at his compatriots, took one more look at Cass, and turned and ran the other direction, calling for backup.

Cass was at the bank of elevators now. She stopped to look back over her shoulder.

"You coming, Zach?" she called across the lobby.

Zach shook off his surprise at this whole series of events and sprinted across the lobby, avoiding the guards that littered the floor.

Cass smoothly inserted her key card into the marked slot and pushed the "up" arrow. They waited nonchalantly for a few seconds, then the elevator arrived.

The door dinged open.

Inside, Maya Krishnamurti was waiting for them.

15

Maya Krishnamurti was a striking woman. As soon as the elevator doors opened it was obvious that she was in command. Her designer heels and sleeveless power dress showed off the shape of her calves and the size of her biceps. Her raven hair hung straight to her waist. She looked like some wild but successful fusion of a Fortune 500 CEO and a prize fighter.

Maya stepped out of the elevator and displaced Cass and Zach with the sheer force of her presence. High-end tablet glowing in hand, she waved off the knot of guards who'd come running from deeper in the building.

"That will be all, gentleman," she said with her Mumbai-born accent. "I will take it from here."

Zach was staring. Cass gave him an elbow to the ribs.

Maya tapped and swiped at the tablet and the alarms went silent. Cass guessed that she was probably in her early forties but, remembering that many of the people in the building were probably among the

Turned, decided that she had no idea how old this woman might actually be. Her blazing white teeth did look a little pointy.

After Maya had dispensed with the guards and the alarm, she turned her full attention to Cass and Zach. She had three or four inches on Cass and her stilettos almost put her eye to eye with Zach. She scanned them each from head to toe and back again, sizing them up.

"I can see why he likes you," Maya said to Cass with a raised eyebrow. Then, gesturing toward the sword slung on her back, she added, "Just the *idea* of a 'single, Asian female with doctoral training, wandering eye, and razor sharp sword' would doubtless put some starch in his pants."

Maya made some kind of note in her tablet, then looked Zach in the eye.

"You," she said with a mix of derision and sympathy, "are clearly the cute side-kick destined to never get the girl."

Zach started to protest but she cut him off. She was already headed back to the elevator, waving for them to follow her, heels clicking smartly on the marble floor.

Cass and Zach joined her in the elevator. The tube rocketed upward and, after the first few floors, opened onto an external view of the city. The scene, though, wasn't what Cass had expected. Rather than looking out onto the Underside hub through which they'd entered, a view of London unfolded before them. It was late afternoon but the sun, low on the horizon, was still bright. The city gleamed.

Maya tapped and swiped a few more times, then, without looking up, held out her hand to Cass, beckoning with two manicured fingers for the return of the stolen key card. Cass grudgingly handed it over. Maya tucked it away and, absorbed in whatever other problems she was simultaneously handling, continued to ignore them.

In surprisingly short order, the elevator came to a smooth stop and the doors opened onto a penthouse suite with high, arching ceilings. One entire wall was two stories of glass, framing a view of London centered on the Thames and the Tower of London. A massive mahogany desk that must have been hundreds of years old anchored the room. The room, in general, embodied this same hybridity: the architecture was all steel, concrete, and glass, while the furniture, rugs, and bar looked like they'd been enjoyed for centuries.

Richard York was standing next to the wall of glass in gray slacks and a black turtleneck, his back to the elevator. His silhouette was dramatically backlit by the setting sun so that Cass and Zach had to shade their eyes with one hand in order to look directly at him.

Zach shook his head. "Figures," he said under his breath, "the guy isn't just alive, he's been resurrected as a sun-god."

"Yes," Maya said loudly, signaling their arrival to Richard, "Apollo will see you now."

Richard was surprised by their arrival. Evidently, he'd been honestly lost in thought, not just posing by the window. When he turned stiffly toward them, they could immediately see that he wasn't the same man they'd known before. His shoulders were bowed, one arm was still in a sling, the other leaned on a cane, and a wicked new scar traversed the bridge of his nose.

But Cass could also see, even from the across the room, that he was struggling to control his emotions at the sight of her. Still backlit by the sun, his face shaded, he took her in for a moment, eyes hungry as his mouth opened slightly in an involuntary gasp. Then, quickly gathering himself, he closed his eyes as his features shifted into a calm, cool expression.

"Cassandra," he said, nodding in her direction. "Zach."

Involuntarily, Cass took a handful of steps toward him, her hand slightly extended at the sight of his injuries. Zach stepped closer and gently took her by the arm—not as if he were trying hold her back, but as if he were urging her to be careful.

Maya watched the whole tableau with her characteristic mix of detached amusement, rational assessment, and mild sympathy.

"Richard," Cass said. "I didn't know you were alive. And I didn't dare believe it when they told me."

She stopped, not sure what to say next. She could sense deep within herself a storm of violent emotions—relief, anger, and desire mingling together—but when she tried to give in to them, they receded, blocked off behind that interior door inside her, dim and distant. The result left Cass uncertain, and stuck. Richard waited. The ten yards or so between them felt like both a very short distance—practically nothing—and an unbridgeable divide.

The silence grew heavier. Cass settled for something honest but banal. "I'm glad you're okay."

Richard returned the sentiment. "I feel the same. I'm glad to see that you are also well," adding, after a beat, "and you, too, Zach."

"I have a thousand questions," Cass said, the ice broken. She pulled free of Zach's gentle grip and started across the room toward Richard. The words came flooding out. "Did you see what happened with Judas? How did you survive? Why didn't you contact me? Why leave me in the cold? What is going on with the Lost? Who is their new leader? Are you going to be okay?"

She was close to him now, close enough to reach out and touch him. They were both beautifully framed by the setting sun in a way that made Zach both squint and wince. Cass reached out to touch his broken arm or the scar on his nose, her hand hovering indecisively in the air without making contact.

"Why did you run away?" she asked.

Richard didn't answer. But, as if in confirmation of the fact that he had run away, he turned aside and limped toward the bar to pour himself a drink.

"Cassandra," he started, taking a sip from his crystal tumbler, "I'm sorry. This is all much more complicated than you know."

He took a long pull from his drink, finishing it off, and set the glass back down on the bar with a little too much force.

"I can't, however, explain things right now. I didn't want you to see me like this, tottering around the room like an old man. And, more to the point, we don't have much time today. Company is reported to be on its way —evidently, they followed you here."

Richard looked at Maya for confirmation of this point. She glanced down at her tablet and then nodded gravely.

"Things are spinning out of control," Richard continued. "With Judas gone, the old order is collapsing and the old rules no longer apply. The Lost are growing wild and reckless. Their new leader hasn't yet succeeded in uniting all the factions." He paused. "In the old days, something like this would never have happened."

"Something like . . . what?" Cass asked.

Richard ignored her question and continued, keeping a safe distance between them. "For the moment," he said, "what I *can* do is to help you retrieve that relic. I can help you retrieve the chains of St. Paul from the basilica in Rome."

Zach looked ready to decline that offer, but Richard dismissed him with a glance and turned his attention back to Cass.

"I'm in no condition to help you myself, but I'm going to send my oldest friend and most talented partner with you. She will help you in any way you ask."

Richard looked past Cass to Maya. "Maya, go with them. Help however you can. Make sure they get whatever they need to secure the relic and find Miranda."

Maya's mouth opened in surprise, but she quickly recovered, set her jaw, and pressed her lips together in a thin, determined line.

Cass didn't know whether to object like Zach or be surprised like Maya. In the end, she didn't have a chance to decide how she ought to react.

At that same moment, alarms began to flash and a feminine, disembodied voice calmly informed them over the loudspeakers that building security had been breached.

16

THE SUN HAD sunk below the horizon, fading into red. The emergency lights now strobed the same bloody color. The soothing, automated voice that had sounded the alarm continued to drone on: "Warning, perimeter breach. Warning, perimeter breach."

Before she knew what she'd done, Cass's sword was in her hand and she'd pivoted to put her back to Zach's. Richard stayed right where he was, alert but unconcerned. Maya made a beeline for the private elevator in the far corner of the room, making sure it was ready at a moment's notice.

Only a few seconds after the alarm sounded, the main office doors burst open and a heavily armed security squad swept into the room, checking corners and securing perimeters. The squad consisted entirely of women. They were each more than six feet tall. They balked at the sight of Cass with her drawn sword, but Richard waved them off.

Figures that Richard's private security detail would consist entirely of Amazons, Cass thought to herself, annoyed at their competence.

"What's the situation, Captain," Richard asked.

The captain put a finger to the earpiece concealed in her ear and reported back: "Ten feral Lost, two groups of five that breached the building in two separate locations. They do, in fact, appear to be hunting for Ms. Jones. But we still need to move you to a secure location, sir, ASAP."

"Yes, in a moment, Captain. I'm sure, though, that this isn't anything you can't handle. We need to conclude our business here, first."

Richard pulled out his phone and, while composing a message, his thumbs flying, called across the room to Maya. "You will take care of them, Maya? You will help them secure the relic?"

The first time he'd brought this up, it had sounded like an order. This time, though, it sounded like a request, like he was entrusting her with something of personal significance to him, calling on her loyalty and friendship.

"I've got this, Richard," Maya said. "No need to worry."

Richard finished his message and pushed send. Maya's tablet lit up with a set of instructions and research materials.

"Cass, Zach," Maya called. "It's time to go." The private elevator doors swished opened. Maya stepped in and held the door with her hand.

Cass took a long look at Richard. She decided to trust him—and, by extension, to trust Maya.

"Let's go, Zach," Cass said. She took him by the elbow and they moved quickly across the room.

"Godspeed," Richard said, just before one of the main doors was blown off its hinges and a handful of feral Lost, greeted with gunfire, loped into the room. Before anyone knew what had happened, a pair of Richard's security team were down. Cass, looking back, stopped in her tracks, sword raised, ready to return to help.

"Go!" Richard shouted, unsheathing a long, thin blade from the shaft of his cane. As one of the Lost leapt in his direction he sidestepped the attack and, with an elegant swing of his blade, sent its head rolling. The body dissolved into white ash.

"Go," Richard said to Cass, quietly this time, as if they were standing eye to eye, rather than separated by the whole room.

Cass went.

Richard's security bundled him off toward a safe room, sporadic gunfire covering their escape. Maya was still waiting, holding the elevator doors at bay. Zach got there first, but Cass wasn't far behind. However, one of the Lost was also right on her heels. As soon as Cass cleared the elevator doors, Maya slipped her hand away from the door and hit a button for the basement level. They stood waiting for the doors to close as the feral vampire bore down on them. Just as Cass began to worry that the doors would be too slow, they swept cleanly shut, and the leaping vampire crashed heavily into the far side.

The elevator smoothly accelerated downward as if nothing had happened. Zach let out a breath he didn't know he'd been holding, Cass lowered her sword, and Maya calmly watched the floors tick off as they rushed toward their destination.

When they reached the designated subbasement, the doors dinged open. Cass found herself in a space that was part locker room, part military-style ops center, and part train station. Lockers with clothes and gear lined one wall. A bank of computers and surveillance monitors lined another. And, on the far end, some kind of rocket-sled was positioned on tracks leading into the darkness of a narrow, circular tunnel.

"Alriiight," Cass said to exaggerated effect, "I see you've got your own secret base down here—hidden away under the office tower that disguises your other, normal secret base."

Cass and Zach shared a look and almost laughed.

Cass tamped the laugh down and just finished up with a half-admiring: "Pretty cool."

"Excuse me for just a moment," Maya said, heading to the lockers. "My original schedule for the day didn't call for any tactical gear."

Maya punched a code into one of the lockers and surveyed the gear inside. Then, without any wasted time or fuss, she unzipped her dress and stepped out of it. She was, Cass and Zach could plainly see, absolutely ripped.

Cass gulped and stared. This time, Zach had to give *her* an elbow to the ribs.

Maya stepped into a pair of black pants and boots, then shrugged into a sleeveless top. Everything fit like a glove. Apparently, even her emergency, "secret mission" clothes were tailored. She picked a jacket from among several and zipped her tablet into a pre-packed go-bag.

"Okay," Maya said, evidently familiar enough with slack-jawed stares that they no longer registered, "to the sled."

The sled had four seats. Maya slipped into the "driver's" seat and booted up the controls while Cass and Zach crawled into the back. The sled's systems cycled online and a power meter slowly rose from red to yellow toward green.

"Buckle up," Maya said as a couple of Lost tore through the roof of the elevator, dropped to the floor, and rushed the room.

But before the pair could get their bearings, the system flashed green, Maya punched the "go" button, and they were all three flattened into their seats by the force of their acceleration.

17

CASS WASN'T SURE if "rocket-sled" was the appropriate technical term for what they were riding in, but the fact that it was basically a sled and literally rocketing down a tube clinched it for her: it was a rocket-sled.

The force of their acceleration was enormous. Clearly, it was built for emergency evacuations not daily pleasure trips. As soon as the system engaged and Maya punched "go," it felt like an enormous, fat hand had reached out of the ether to smash her flat into her seat. She had a hard time even turning her head to see if Zach was okay. When she finally did, she saw that he was also pinned in his seat, struggling to fasten his seatbelt.

When, out of the corner of his eye, Zach saw her looking at him, he grimaced exaggeratedly, drawing his lips into a thin line. Encouraged by a glimpse of Cass's smile, he upped the ante and opened his mouth in a huge smile that captured the full force of the wind and blew his cheeks out like a windsock, revealing his teeth and gums. Bug-eyed, he looked like an inflated balloon.

Cass lost it. All the stress and pressure that had been building for the past few hours burst in a peal of laughter and, when she opened her own mouth to laugh, she ended up creating the same comical effect. Zach, in response, also lost it. This only wound them up further, creating a feedback loop of laughter and rubbery cheeks.

Cass couldn't tell if the tears streaming down her face were a product of the wind or her laughter or just the remnant of emotional release. She struggled to calm down and catch her breath but, helpless not to look again, she turned her head back in Zach's direction only to discover that a new face, pointy incisors bared, had also joined them.

Cass's laughter turned into a shout of surprise that Zach, when he also discovered the vampire hanging onto the back of the sled, echoed.

Bastard, Cass thought. *Stupid vampires ruin everything.*

She tried to raise her hand to punch him in the face and knock him loose, but she could hardly lift her arm. The thing must have been incredibly strong to not only hang on to the sled but inch its way forward.

Zach, drawing a lesson from Cass's failed punch, tried using his elbow instead. With a more compact, g-force friendly gesture, he cracked his elbow into the creature's nose, splintering it into a bloody mess.

But the vampire's grip didn't loosen. In fact, he just seemed angrier now as he unleashed a wild snarl. He struck back at Zach, raking a razor sharp set of nails across Zach's chest, hooking a finger under his shirt collar. Zach cried out in pain and alarm.

Screw this, Cass decided. *This is your stop, pal.*

Cass unbuckled her seatbelt, shimmied down into her seat, and flipped around so that her shoulders were planted on the floor and her feet were pointed up. Gathering herself, she kicked the vampire with both feet, connecting with his face.

The vampire lost his grip on the sled and it looked, for a moment, like he was going to tumble free of the sled and into the darkness of the tunnel. Instead, now he just flapped in the air like a streamer attached to the sled, two fingers of one hand still hooked under Zach's collar.

Zach screamed again, fighting to break free. There wasn't much Cass could do—flapping in the breeze, the vampire was out of her reach.

Maya looked back to see what all the screaming was about. When she saw that Cass was upside down on the floor and Zach was flying a vampire like a kite, she shook her head, scolding them like she was the only real adult on this rocket-sled. Maya, unlike the rest of them, appeared unaffected by the speed. Her hair looked great and the striking features of her face were still beautifully composed. In one easy motion she pulled a 9mm Glock from a holster under the dash and fired a silver bullet right between the vampire's eyes and, for good measure, a second into his heart. The body dissolved into ash and instantly disappeared in the wind.

"Thanks," Zach shouted into the wind.

"You are welcome," Maya returned.

Cass struggled to right herself in her seat and, with exaggerated care, rebuckled her seatbelt.

They continued down the tube for another five minutes before the sled pulled to a stop. Cass was pretty sure that it would take a couple of days before her cheeks returned to their normal shape. Zach was patting down his own face, checking to see if everything had returned to its prior position.

Maya swung elegantly out of the sled, go-bag in hand, and looked back at the two of them, subtly shaking her head in some mix of wonder and disapproval at their antics. This almost set Zach and Cass to laughing again.

"Children," Maya said, "it is time to move along."

From there, Maya led them up an ancient, narrow, twisting flight of stairs. The stone steps had deep grooves worn in them. Cass guessed that the passage was at least five hundred years old. They climbed five or six stories worth of stairs, Maya in front, Zach in the middle, Cass in the back. Zach tried hard to keep his eyes on the uneven, stone stairs and not on Maya's perfectly toned glutes. Cass also tried hard to keep her eyes on the stairs and not on Zach's own toned buttocks. They both suspected that Maya wouldn't have had the same problem if she were bringing up the rear.

Finally, though, the stairs ended at a heavy wooden door on black iron hinges. Maya disabled the lock and leaned against the door, shoving it open. They stepped out from the stairs and onto a grass covered hill. The night sky was full of stars and Rome lay spread out below them.

"There," Maya said, pointing out a particular section of the city, "is the Basilica of Saint Paul's Outside the Walls. That's where we'll find the relic we're looking for."

18

THEY MADE THEIR way down into the city on foot. Maya seemed to know exactly where they were headed. But, as far as Cass could tell, she wasn't leading them directly to the Basilica. That wouldn't have made much sense anyway in the middle of the night. Instead, Maya lead them through narrow streets into an old section of the city to a second story apartment. They climbed the exterior stairs up the side of the house. Maya punched a code into the shabby door's high-end security system and ushered them inside.

"Welcome to tonight's safe house," Maya said drily.

After they were all inside, Maya swung the door shut with a satisfying "thunk"—the door must have been solid steel, disguised as ratty wood from the outside—and armed the security system. Cass was surprised at how relieved she felt to be locked securely behind a steel door. Now that they were safe, the stress and exhaustion of the past day caught up with her and she slumped onto a lumpy sofa.

Zach sat down at the small kitchen table, either his bones or the chair creaking as he settled gingerly into it. Maya checked the kitchen for supplies and took a look in the apartment's one other room, a bedroom with a pair of twin beds. Then she fished her tablet from her go-bag, set it on the table, and unpacked some of the rest of her gear in the bedroom.

Cass and Zach looked at each other from across the room. They were both too tired to move. Cass groaned, her voice low and gravely. Zach joined in, harmonizing his groan with her pitch and timbre. Still groaning, Cass rested her head on the back of the sofa and looked at the water stained ceiling. Zach rested his forehead on the kitchen table as he exhaled a deep breath of exhaustion, examining the grain of the wood at close range. They continued groaning and sighing in concert for almost a minute until Maya popped her head out of the bedroom, eyebrow raised, to see what was going on. They both stopped instantly and looked at her innocently. Maya went back to what she'd been doing. As soon as she was gone, they couldn't resist a quiet snicker that, given how tired they were, felt good and quickly faded.

"I'm hungry," Cass said. "What have we got to eat over there Zach?"

Zach leaned back in his chair and took a look in the fridge. Then, wiggling his chair toward the counter, he looked inside the cupboards. Except for condiments, the fridge was basically empty. The cupboards were full of dusty cans. Zach grabbed a can of chili from the nearest shelf, blew the dust off the top, and leaned forward to inspect the label.

"It looks like we've got a lot of canned chili, expiration date . . . two years ago. Though I'm pretty sure this stuff lasts forever" Zach said, shaking the can as if to hear what was inside. The can made an unusual glurping sound. He tossed it onto the couch next to her. "For what it's worth, this one *sounds* good."

Cass looked at it suspiciously, but didn't touch it. She squeezed a little farther into the corner of the couch, putting a little more distance between herself and the can. The can of chili made another glurping sound, this time all on its own, and Cass got up from the couch to have a look in the cupboards for herself. Behind a row of cans, she found a vacuum sealed bag of pistachios.

"Aha!" she said, claiming victory.

Zach looked skeptical, doubting that a bag of pistachios warranted any celebration. Cass sat down next to him and, just as Maya returned, busted the bag open, scattering nuts across the table. Cass scooped the nuts back toward herself. Maya, clearing a few nuts off her tablet, sat down with them.

"The chains of Saint Paul are housed in the *Basilica Papale San Paolo Fuori le Mure*," Maya said with a perfect Italian accent.

"Yeah," Cass added, "they're usually displayed in a glass case on an altar in the chapel of relics in the basilica. The chapel is open to the public on a daily basis.

The altar sits atop an underground tombstone and sarcophagus associated with Paul."

Maya tapped, swiped, and brought up on her tablet several images of the basilica, the chapel, and the chains.

Cass continued. "The chains are, according to tradition, the ones that held the apostle Paul during his trial in Rome. If Judas was telling the truth, then, regardless of their actual provenance, they have doubtless been invested by belief and tradition with enormous power over centuries of veneration."

Zach nodded. Cass split open a couple of pistachio shells, popped the nuts in her mouth, and then tried, unsuccessfully, to suck the red stains from tips of her fingers. Giving up, she cracked a couple more. Zach furtively gathered up the mess of discarded shells for her as she went.

"The security guarding this relic is not imposing," Maya said. "If it were just a question of bypassing several security guards, some alarms, and a glass case, we could be in and out tonight. The problem is that the relic is protected by a powerful spell that is especially geared to keep vampires at bay. This, of course, is where you come in, Cass, and why Amare needs your help to acquire them."

Cass popped a couple more pistachios open and, before Zach could clean up the mess, she swept the shells off the table into his lap with the back of her hand.

"The trouble," Cass said, "is that I don't actually know anything about spells. I only know about relics. I'm not sure how I can help."

"Yes," Zach agreed, picking bits of shell out of his lap, "that's true. But spells like this are always built around the history and characteristics of the relics themselves. So it's not just a matter of undoing a spell, it's a matter of undoing a spell that is keyed to the history of the relic itself."

"Right," Maya said, taking back control of the conversation. She tapped, swiped and displayed the tablet again, this time showing the text of spell, written in Latin. Only one piece appeared to be missing. "We know the basic outlines of the spell-breaker, but this missing element—here—is keyed to the relic's history, to a specific detail that we have yet to recover."

Cass leaned in close, tilted the tablet toward herself for a better look, and left a red smudge on the screen. She quickly read through the Latin text under her own breath.

"I can already tell what the missing piece *should* be," Cass said, "but I don't know how to fill in the blank off the top of my head. I do know, though, that there is a small, private library located near the basilica that houses just the kind of information we'll need. I think that's where we should start tomorrow."

"Agreed," Maya said approvingly. Cass was surprised at how good it felt to receive approval for having obscure academic knowledge. Her time as a grad student seemed like a completely different life now.

Still, it was nice to feel like some part of her former life was still relevant and useful to her current one.

Cass smiled. Maya eyed her, head slightly cocked to one side as if she was still assessing Cass. She then continued: "We should get some rest and then try first thing in the morning."

Maya paused, as if waiting for them to fill in the next obvious blank in their conversation. She looked at them both, lingering for a moment at Cass's wayward eye, then explained, "There are only two beds in the bedroom."

Cass and Maya both turned to Zach.

Zach put up his hands in a defensive gesture. "What? I definitely don't need *both* the beds," he teased.

"Right," Maya said, "I am glad to hear you agree. Cass and I will share the room and you will sleep out here."

19

WITH THAT, THE evening came to an abrupt end. Maya repacked her bag and Cass crashed on a creaky twin mattress. Zach found an extra blanket in the closet and made himself a bed on the living room floor. Maya turned out the lights and, within sixty seconds of lying down, was gently snoring.

Dim light from a street lamp cast a shadow through the blinds and onto the wall above Cass's bed. Cass lay in bed for a long time, staring at the bars of light and shadow, exhausted but not sleeping. Her emotions, unsettled, rattled their cages. Every time she closed her eyes, rather than seeing darkness, Cass would see the unmarked door they'd passed after descending the stairs into the Underside. The image was sharp and vivid. She could almost feel the door's lock, bright and cold and solid, under the tips of her fingers.

The previous night's twelve hours of rest now seemed like an impossibly distant miracle. How had she done it? How had she finally slept after months of torment?

What was different?

Zach.

The answer was Zach.

Cass grabbed her pillow and tiptoed out to the front room. Maya continued to snore. Zach also looked to be asleep. Cass settled onto the floor behind him, balling up her pillow and slipping an arm around his waist. The zoo of emotions in her head quieted down. Her guilt over Richard's supposed death, the loss she'd been struggling both to feel and move past, and her growing desire for Zach's steady presence in her life stopped fighting with each other. She felt an honest hush of gratitude and acceptance take hold. She squeezed Zach tighter, snuggling close. Everything in her head went silent.

Zach rolled toward her, mumbling something, his eyes half open, pulling her close.

The second time he tried to say it, Cass made out what he was whispering.

"I'm sorry, Cass. About Richard. I'm sorry I didn't say anything. They were wrong to ask me to keep it a secret. And I was wrong to go along with it . . ."

Cass didn't answer. She didn't want to sort out feelings she couldn't quite feel. She knew that underneath her relief at Richard's reappearance, she was also incredibly angry at the deception. But it wasn't just Zach. Ultimately, it was Richard's choice not to let her know he was alive. And that choice cut her deeply.

So she pressed a finger to Zach's lips to silence him. He hesitated for a moment—but when she left her pistachio-stained finger on his lips, he kissed it. Then kissed it again. Cass leaned in and returned his kiss, her hand slipping beneath his torn shirt, resting in the small of his back. She bit his lip, lightly, playfully. He tucked her dark hair behind her ear. He pulled her closer, gently, his arm around her waist. He held her as if with one wrong move, he might shatter her. His hand settled low on her hip, his thumb hooked inside the waistband of her jeans, trying to hang on.

She kissed him again, fiercely. Her weak eye slipped into focus, softly burning.

Zach forgot his own name.

When he remembered, he opened his eyes again. He was startled by what he saw. Whiffs of radiantly white smoke rose from Cass and swirled around them. He looked directly into her normally cloudy eye, illuminated now from the inside out.

He smiled crookedly at the sight of her glowing. Cass, embarrassed, buried her head in his shoulder, biting her own lip this time.

"Zach," she said.

"Cass," he returned, waiting.

Cass didn't know what to say next. They enjoyed the silence.

"Just rest, Cass," Zach said. "Just rest, now."

Her eyelids were heavy. She mumbled a response. She wrapped Zach around her like a blanket and slipped almost immediately into a deep sleep. Zach folded her even more tightly into his arms and joined her.

They slept without interruption until the morning.

Cass slept without stirring until she woke with a start when something sharp scratched her bare ankle. The morning sun had already flooded the room with light. She could feel a hot line of blood welling on her ankle. Cass forced herself to lie perfectly still.

Whatever had scratched her, it wasn't Zach.

20

ATLANTIS WAS PURRING and batting Cass's leg with his paw. How the cat had gotten to Rome or into a locked room—these were things Cass wasn't sure she wanted to know. Atlantis came and went as he pleased. Apart from Cass, he lived a mysterious life all his own. Cass, though, was always happy to see him.

Cass reached down and scooped him up, burying her face deep in his fur. He reminded her of home. Zach mumbled something about being late for his third period biology class and fell silent again, his arm still around Cass.

"Hmmm," Maya said from the bedroom door, already dressed and ready to go. She surveyed the scene: Zach snuggling Cass snuggling Atlantis. "I do hope sleeping together on the living room floor also actually involved getting some sleep. We have got a busy day ahead of us."

Zach jerked awake, his cheeks flushing a crimson red. He started to protest but Atlantis squirmed free of Cass and started batting at his nose like a ball of string.

Zach stumbled to the bathroom and Cass tidied up the mess, folding blankets, moving couches, and making beds. While Zach was still in the shower, a delivery boy showed up with coffee and biscotti. When Zach rejoined them, Cass took her turn in the shower.

It was hard to say what last night had meant. Cass and Zach were hesitant to make eye contact. They gathered up their gear. The tension between them was subtle but palpable.

While Cass and Zach were waiting awkwardly on the small landing at the top of the stairs to the apartment, Maya was still inside, shutting everything down. As Zach started to whistle, studying the clouds in the morning sky, Cass decided this wasn't going to work. They couldn't just pretend to go back to the ways things had been before. And whatever her feelings for Richard, she couldn't ignore the very real way in which Zach grounded her, and the way she was coming to need and desire him.

I'm choosing, she realized. Seeing Richard had released something inside her: a mixture of guilt and desire with a dash of fantasy and yes, even love, would continue to run its course, but she would no longer allow it to control her choices. *And I'm choosing Zach.*

"Zach," she said, taking his hand and calling for his attention.

"It's okay, Cass . . ." he said, looking over her shoulder.

"That's not what I'm trying to say," Cass responded, pressing him back against the door and kissing him again. The kiss went on long enough that Maya had to rattle the door knob and ask to please be let out of the apartment. When she finally got through the door, Zach, rather than blushing again, just beamed. Maya couldn't help but offer a small eye roll, but she was glad for the improved vibe.

They hurried out to the street where Maya had a car waiting for them. Atlantis jumped free of Cass as they got into the car, but Cass was pretty sure that, on several occasions along their route, she spotted him weaving through the crowded sidewalks, following them.

The driver left them off at the Basilica of Saint Paul Outside the Walls but they weren't actually aiming to see the chains yet. First, they needed to track down the missing element of the spell-breaker. Cass led them around the corner of the basilica and down a narrow side street. The small, private library they needed was a couple of blocks away. The library was a small, two story building, a nondescript converted house. A small wooden sign, written in Latin, hung neatly from an iron rod above the door: *Bibliotheca Mysteria*.

Cass stopped at the door, trying to decide if they were supposed to knock first. Maya, though, brushed past Cass and walked right in. Cass and Zach followed her to find themselves in a small foyer with a few books and artifacts on display and a tiny Italian woman, surely in her seventies with coke-bottle glasses perched on her nose, seated behind a desk. The sign on her desk read: "By Appointment Only."

Maya, in fluent Italian, explained that they needed access to the collection this morning. The old woman, her eyes comically magnified by her thick glasses, looked up at Maya in disbelief. She shook her head and pointed to the sign.

"I'm afraid that's impossible," she said. "The collection can only be seen by appointment."

Maya steeled herself for negotiation. "I understand," she said. "With whom should I speak to make a reservation?"

"I make all the reservations," the woman sternly replied, gripping the appointment book, surprised that anyone would think differently.

"May we have a reservation for this morning," Maya asked, checking her watch, "for the top of the hour?"

The librarian opened her appointment book and scanned through all the appointments for the coming week. The entire page was blank. Then she pointed to the appointment sign.

"Again, I'm afraid that's impossible. As the sign indicates, all appointments must be made a week in advance."

Maya bent close, examining the fine print of the sign. It did indeed say this in tiny letters at the bottom of the sign. Maya looked at the librarian, at the empty appointment book open on the desk, and then back at the librarian. She waited.

"I don't make the rules," the librarian said. "I just follow them. You're welcome to make an appointment for this time next week."

Maya looked like she was struggling to formulate a sufficiently diplomatic response. Her eyes narrowed, her lips pursed, and one vein in her left bicep visibly throbbed.

Zach felt like he'd better jump in with some kind of distraction. He looked down to find Atlantis at his feet, purring and rubbing up against his leg. He gave Cass a nudge, picked up the cat, and started to loudly praise the cat's beauty.

"Awww, what a bweautiful kitty-witty cat," he exclaimed, stroking Atlantis between the ears and drawing the librarian's attention away from Maya. The distraction was surprisingly effective. At the sight of Atlantis, a look of horror crossed the librarian's face.

"What on earth do you think you're doing, young man!" she half-shouted, half-sneezed. "Get that filthy animal out of here!"

She grabbed a broom from behind the desk and went after Zach and the cat with surprising speed, as if she intended to either sweep them away or beat them over the head. She looked ready to do whichever was necessary.

Zach started backing away toward the door, all the while going on and on in his sing-song voice about "not hurting bweautiful kitty-witties." The more he cooed and backpedaled around the room, the angrier the librarian became.

Cass, meanwhile, could take a hint. She grabbed Maya by the elbow and, as the librarian sneezed and took an actual swing at Zach's head, the two of them slipped quietly into the special collections room behind the desk. The room was gorgeous. It was filled with floor to ceiling shelves, books, reading tables, lamps, rich carpets, and the heady scent of yellowed paper and worn leather. Cass's heart leapt: there were few things in the world she loved more than old books.

"Okay," Cass said, trying to focus on their situation, "now what? That distraction isn't going to last long. She'll have Zach bruised and out the door any minute. We'll never find what we're looking for in time."

"True," Maya said. "But it is also the case that what we are looking for is unlikely to be found in this part of the collection. We do not just need access to the special collection, we need access to the . . . special special collection."

With that, Maya pulled a funky, three-pronged key from her bag with the head of an actual skeleton cast on one end. She headed for a side door and took a look inside. It appeared to be a broom closet. She shut the door again, inserted the key, and turned it an entire three hundred and sixty degrees.

When she opened the door a second time, a deep, golden light shone out.

"*This* is the room we need," Maya said.

Cass stepped through the door and found herself in a vast, Gothic room with a bank of stained glass windows on one end, framed by arches and lit by torches, with shelves of books receding upward and outward into the darkness.

21

THE LIGHT FILTERING through the stained glass was weak and came from a low angle. Rather than morning, it felt like early evening. It felt like twilight.

"We're in the Underside," Cass deduced.

"Very good," Maya said. "Often, there are, in very old places like this, little pockets of the Underside adjacent to the everyday world or forgotten passages leading from one world to the other. These spaces aren't always stable and, sometimes, they move of their own accord, slipping from one neighboring space to another. Sometimes, like a bubble, they just pop and disappear altogether."

Cass craned her neck backward, trying to take in the size of the space while also remembering that, in the everyday world, all of this fit in a broom closet.

"I don't know how I'll even begin to sort through the books we have here," Cass said, cowed by the undefined size of the stacks receding into the darkness. "It could take days for me to just get my bearings, and weeks of research after that to gather the obscure information about Paul that we'd need for the missing element of the spell-breaker."

Cass trailed her hand along the spines of a row of leather-bound books, scanning the mostly Greek, Latin, and Arabic titles.

Maya smiled. "In this place, I think we may be able to take a more direct route. Are you familiar with a lost text called 'The Gospel According to St. Paul'?"

"Yeah," Cass said, "I've heard of it. But no one has read it. It's been lost for almost two thousand years. Many scholars doubt there is such a thing. Its existence is only mentioned in a handful of apocryphal texts."

Cass's attention snagged on the cover of a book she'd just stumbled across on the shelf: Aristotle's book on Comedy, the lost second half of his *Poetics*. She reached to pull it off the shelf but Maya, from behind, constrained her arm and gently pointed her face in a different direction. Her touch was firm but inviting. Cass felt a pleasant, electric shock travel down her spine as Maya whispered into her ear: "Not today, my dear. Not today. What *we* need is over there."

Maya smiled and pointed at an old fashioned card catalogue, straight out of the fifties, positioned beneath a torch on the other side of the room.

"This is how we find the book we need. The book is somewhere in this labyrinth of stacks. The catalogue is the key to those stacks. The trick, though, is that an extremely valuable book like Paul's Gospel is unlikely to just have a card of its own. But, if we're lucky, we should be able to decode its location from a couple of other cards."

Maya stooped down to examine the labels on the different card catalogue drawers. Cass watched over her shoulder. Maya ran her finger from one drawer to the next and stopped abruptly at the top of the third row.

"This is the one," Maya said, sliding her finger into the drawer's rounded brass handle.

But when she pulled, nothing happened. She tried again, pulling harder. Still nothing. The drawer was wedged in place.

"There is no way this damn drawer will have the better of me," Maya threatened. She slid her index finger back into the brass handle and pulled, her triceps in sharp relief. When the handle itself began to bow outward, Cass feared that she'd just pull the handle clean off and leave the drawer intact. But before the handle could snap, the drawer came loose all at once. It came flying out of its slot, scattering a thousand manually typed index cards into the air.

"Mother!" Maya swore as the cards went airborne, swirling around them like a blizzard of fat, flat snowflakes.

Cass, though, didn't panic. The moment the cards came loose, Cass felt a deep calm settle over her. The truth was that they couldn't afford to fail at this. Miranda was in danger and they needed to act fast. They needed to find her.

And, especially, the truth was that *Cass* needed to find her.

Cass flashed on a memory of Miranda, graveside at Rose's funeral, pulling Cass close and kissing her on the forehead. When the image flashed in her mind, Cass felt a small, white fire flicker and ignite in her head.

Time slowed to crawl, but Cass could still move freely. Unhurried, she stepped into the eye of the blizzard. Her weak eye wandered of its own accord from one card to the next, reading each of them as they fluttered by.

"Here," she said to herself, plucking a card from the air. "This one."

She pinched a second and a third between her thumb and index finger. "And this one. And this one."

She wasn't entirely sure what she was looking for, but when she saw a card they needed, it clearly stood out from the rest. It gave off a faint glow. Cass turned slowly in a circle, her wandering eye still scanning each card.

She plucked a fourth card from the air, then bent low to look more closely at a final card, already close to the ground. "And this one," she finished, snagging the fifth.

Once she had all five cards in hand, time snapped back into its regular shape and the remaining cards that had, a moment ago, been suspended in the air, crashed to the ground in a heap, covering the stone floor in chaotic layers of white index cards.

Cass fanned out all five cards in her hand and held them up for Maya like she'd just been dealt the winning hand in poker.

Maya wasn't entirely sure what she'd just seen. Her jaw was slack and her full lips formed a quizzical "O."

Cass gave her a small smile. "What? I'm the Seer. Evidently I can do things like that."

Cass spread the cards out on a nearby table and they took a careful look at them. The cards didn't appear to have any clearly common features. Their subjects, authors, and dates of composition were wildly diverse.

Maya flipped one of the cards over. A three digit number ran down the side of the card. She flipped the rest of the cards and, along varying edges, each card had a similar set of digits. Cass chewed on her lip, looking for the right configuration. She reached past Maya and rearranged the cards into a star-shaped pattern. Organized this way, the numbers flowed from the edge of one card to the next, forming an unbroken sequence.

"That's it," Maya said.

At a glance, Cass memorized the number. She grabbed a torch from the wall and, with Maya in tow, began to work her way back into the stacks, orienting herself to the system that organized the collection.

About eight rows back, she turned down an aisle on their left, and hopped onto a wheeled ladder mounted to the shelves. Like she was riding a scooter, she rolled herself down the aisle. About halfway down, she dragged the toe of her boot, bringing the ladder to a stop. She climbed several rungs up the ladder, pulled a slim manuscript from the shelf, and jumped off the ladder from there, landing lightly on her feet.

"Bingo," Cass said, holding up the book.

As they hurried back through the door into the Overside library, Maya and Cass could hear Zach lecturing the librarian on proper feline feces disposal techniques. Atlantis mewed helpfully in the background. Cass peeked around the corner to see the poor librarian slumped in her chair, sneezing, head bowed down atop her desk in defeat. She didn't see them as they quietly crossed to the front door.

"For the last time, young man, you must leave. Leave out this door. And leave the door open." The librarian's voice rasped, her throat red and raw from the sudden onset of a truly miserable allergy attack.

Zach glanced at Cass, who nodded at the slim book under her arm in return. Without another word, he scooped up Atlantis and followed them out the door.

22

IT WAS PAST midnight. Cass, Zach, and Maya, clad in black, slipped along the side of the basilica where the chains of St. Paul were secured and displayed. They were looking for the side door used by priests and caretakers. This entrance would get them close to the chapel of relics.

The night was cloudy, starless, and dark. They shuffled along in the darkness until Maya found what she needed to locate first—the point at which the basilica's security system connected with the city's electrical and information infrastructure—and she stopped without warning. Cass, following Maya, ran right into her. And Zach, following Cass, then ran right into her. They ended up in a noisy, tangled pile of arms and legs, half caught in a bush.

"Damn amateurs," Maya hissed, shrugging them off and getting down to work. "Watch where you are going."

Cass and Zach, meanwhile, took their time untangling themselves.

Maya pulled some tools and equipment from her bag and spliced herself into the basilica's security system. With a bit of digital jujitsu, she overrode the alarms and disarmed sensors that governed the chains of St. Paul.

"The digital end of this break-in is the easy part," Maya reminded them. "Breaking the spell will be the difficult part."

Maya popped the side door open and, single file, they stole inside and toward the chapel of relics. The chains of St. Paul were displayed in a glass case, lit by interior lights.

"They're beautiful," Cass whispered, edging around the altar and closer to the case. Even several yards away, she could feel them resonating with more than a thousand years of invested power. She felt powerfully drawn to them but, still a few feet from the case, something that felt like a magnetic field repelled her and she couldn't get any closer.

"Alright, Maya," Cass said, reaching out with her hand to test the field again, "you're up."

Maya took a deep breath, cleared her mind, and repeated the incantation, careful to include the missing element they'd recovered from Paul's lost Gospel. A few sparks of green light leapt from her hand and fizzled out, leaving the field intact. She tried again with the same result.

Cass noticed, then, that something in the room didn't feel right. Something felt off. But before she could say anything, Zach interjected.

"Ladies," Zach said, "may I be of assistance?"

He took a look over Maya's shoulder at the spell-breaking incantation, muttered an "Alrighty, then" once he had grasped the form and details of the spell, cracked his knuckles, and squared himself to the case. He closed his eyes for a moment, bowed his head, clapped his palms together, repeated the incantation, and pushed the palms of his hands outward toward the glass case. A wave of green light surged from his hands and the protective field around the case collapsed.

"Ha!" he shouted, then remembered it was important to keep quiet.

As the green wave of light washed over and through her, Cass felt the small hairs on the back of her neck stand up and goosebumps pimple her arms. She shivered in the incantation's afterglow. Zach clearly knew what he was doing with magic. Why was she surprised? But her feelings were mixed. In addition to the pleasure of the spell's power, the green crackle of magic also left her with a pang of grief. For Cass, magic couldn't help but mean Miranda.

Cass pushed aside her fear for Miranda and helped Maya remove the lid from the case. Zach stood behind them, congratulating himself. "You're welcome, ladies," he joked, brushing imaginary lint from his shoulders and straightening his imaginary tie. Maya reached into the box and retrieved the heavy, iron chains. She bent down and secured the chains in her bag, then patted the pocket of her vest to make sure that she still had the Pauline manuscript.

Zach beamed and Cass couldn't help but smile in return. They'd done it.

Still, something felt off about the room.

They worked their way down the colonnaded hall and back toward the door they'd originally come through. The farther they got from the chapel or relics, the deeper the shadows felt. Part way down the hall, Cass stopped. She had her head cocked to the side, trying to put her finger on what was wrong, when a voice came from the shadows. The voice felt both powerfully familiar and violently strange.

"Thank you for breaking that spell," the voice said. "No vampire—Turned or Lost—could do it."

On cue, a dozen of the Lost stepped into the faint light, surrounding them.

"Now," the voice continued, "hand over the relic."

"Screw that," Maya said, kicking the nearest vampire in the knee and then, with her bare hands, wrenching his arm in a bone-crunching maneuver that left it twisted in the wrong direction.

Maya tossed Cass the bag with the relic. "Run, Cassandra," she said. "And do not look back. I will be right behind you."

Cass slung the bag over her shoulder and took off running. Miranda was what mattered most now.

When a vampire in a red leather jacket—straight from the set of "Thriller"—blocked her path, Cass drew her sword and slid feet first between his legs. With one sweeping stroke, she cleanly severed both legs at the ankles as she passed beneath him. He stood there for a moment, not sure what had happened, then toppled to the floor in a bloody heap, his feet still squarely planted on the floor next to him. Cass looked back for a moment to confirm her suspicion: the moron was, in fact, wearing just one white glove.

Cass scrambled back to her feet and ran again. She could hear Zach behind her and Maya behind him. The only clear path forward led her back to the chapel of relics. She looked around the chapel, searching for an exit. But the only way out now was down.

She leapt a railing with a "Do Not Enter" sign and bolted down a tight set of stairs into the catacombs beneath the basilica. Zach and Maya were right on her heels now. Gunfire from Maya's Glock echoed cacophonously in the tunnel until it was drowned out by a volley of frustrated screams.

Cass took one hard turn, then a second. But she came to a screeching halt when the passageway ended abruptly at Paul's crypt.

The passage was a dead-end.

23

THERE WAS NO place to go. Cass had led them into a cul-de-sac. Zach and Maya barreled around the corner into the same space. They were dismayed by the ashen look on Cass's face.

"Back here," Cass said, signaling that they should take up positions on the far side of the crypt. Cass stationed herself just around the corner from the entrance. She braced herself against the wall, sword pointed toward the corner, level with her own head, ready to impale whoever came careening around the corner next.

She only had to wait a moment. The ploy worked better than she'd expected. A vampire about her size, all black leather straps, buckles, and tassels, ran head first into the blade.

A country Western vampire? Cass wondered.

Cass threw her weight into to blade, pitching the woman to the floor and severed her head. She crumbled into a pile of white ash.

The next one, though, arrived, before Cass could recover and brace herself again. The second vampire blew around the corner and ran right into Cass, knocking them both over. Cass ended up on the bottom, her sword-arm pinned at an awkward angle. This woman was considerably bigger than the last, her mass straining her snakeskin leather to its limits. Cass couldn't help but admire the kind of confidence it took to wear an outfit like that.

The woman grabbed Cass by the shoulders and shook her. Cass hit the woman hard under the chin with the heel of her free hand, snapping the woman's mouth shut and severing the tip of her tongue. The bit tongue fell to the ground and flopped there. They both paused for a moment and looked at it, bewildered, then the woman's eyes went black and she shook Cass again. She banged Cass's head against the stone floor and offered a slurred snarl, ready to sink her bloody teeth into Cass's exposed neck.

BLAM. BLAM.

Maya fired two shots into the vampire's chest and the woman slumped to the floor, injured but not dispatched, trapping Cass beneath her weight.

Maya cleared the corner of the crypt, her pistol aimed at whoever might come around the corner next. When no one did and everything—for the moment—seemed quiet, she reached down with one sleeveless arm, grabbed the vampire by the seat of her snakeskin pants, and hoisted her off of Cass. Cass struggled to her feet, rubbed the back of her head, and buried her sword in the vampire's heart, turning her to ash.

Cass felt a little unsteady on her feet and her vision was blurry. Worse, waves of black emotion—fear, anger, despair—were crashing against the weakening barricades in her heart, threatening to break loose. She staggered back a step, placed a hand on the wall for support, and tried to clear the cobwebs from her head.

Zach was busy looking for another way out. They couldn't go back the way they'd come, but that didn't mean that they were as trapped as they seemed. He closed his eyes and tried to extend his awareness into the space around them, "feeling" for the presence of some kind of adjacent space in the Underside. He felt along the corners of the space behind the crypt, then down along the floor. When he turned back in the direction of the crypt, he stopped.

A faint noise was coming from inside the crypt itself.

"Do you guys hear that?" Zach asked. "Cass, give me a hand with this."

Zach leaned into the crypt, leveraging his weight against its stone lid. It trembled but barely moved. Cass joined him and, together, the stone lid started to slide. They pushed until it crashed off the far side and the crypt yawned open in front of them, pitch black inside.

Zach took Cass by the elbow. "Listen." he said. They both strained to listen.

"Meow," the crypt said.

They both did a double-take as Atlantis jumped out of the crypt and into Cass's arms. Zach took a second, closer look inside the crypt.

"Stairs," Zach said. "There are stairs inside."

Atlantis purred and squirmed in Cass's arms.

"Good work," Maya replied without looking around, her gun still trained on the corner. She backed along the wall toward them.

Cass handed the bag with the relic back to Maya. "Ladies first," Cass said, gesturing with her sword toward the stairs.

As Maya hopped over the lip of the box and down into the stairwell, Atlantis hissed and took a swipe at her. Cass brushed it off, distracted by the thought of what might come around the corner next. Zach, though, noticed.

"Down you go, big boy," Cass said. "Seers bring up the rear."

Zach thought about objecting, but didn't want to waste their time. He jumped into the crypt. Standing a couple of steps deep, he called for Atlantis to make it easier for Cass to swing over the edge. The cat jumped from Cass's arms, by-passing Zach, and disappeared down the stairs into the darkness.

"I see how it is," Zach said, winking at Cass. "I suppose I'll have to be happy with winning one of you over."

Cass gave him a tired smile but, before she could follow him into the darkness, time thickened and slowed. Zach appeared frozen in place, halfway down the stairs.

Stillness. Silence. Then a shattering sound.

"Cassandra," the powerfully familiar and violently strange voice called again, echoing down the hallway. "Cassandra!"

The voice gripped something deep inside of her, rooting Cass to the spot. A rumbling sound filled the hallway—some combination of heavy footsteps, trembling walls, and the grating of metal on stone.

Cass fought to regain control of her body and reenter the flow of time. She forced her legs to move, one step at a time, until she cleared the blind corner. She had to see what was coming. She had to see what was calling her name.

But once she'd turned the corner, it was clear that the monstrous thing that had come into view was *not* what had been calling her name.

The towering monster was misshapen and lopsided. One eye glowed red and the other socket was empty. Rows of razor sharp teeth gnashed in its mouth. One giant arm noisily dragged an enormous axe across the stone floor while the other arm hung shriveled and limp at its side. Its clothes were mostly tattered and moldering, the only exception being a shiny leather vest with the beast's name lovingly embroidered inside a pink heart: "FRED," it said. The monster had the look of some feral, half-dreamed nightmare set free in the waking world.

Cass tightened her grip on her sword and dropped into a defensive stance. She fought to regain control of both her body and her emotions. She didn't see how she could defeat whatever this thing was. Maybe she could just give Zach and Maya time to escape. Hopelessness swelled in her gut, rising like black bile in her throat, but she pushed it down again.

The monster filled almost the entire passageway. Cass decided she'd better seize the advantage before she lost what open ground remained, trapping her in the crypt.

Okay, "Fred." Here we go, Cass thought.

She advanced, sword raised, as the monster swung its axe in a great, looping circle, taking a chunk out of the ceiling and embedding the blade deep in the stone floor. Cass danced to the side, avoiding the swing, ducked under the haymaker that followed, and cleanly severed the thing's limp and shriveled arm with her sword. The monster cried out in alarm and pain, its voice pitched high and innocent like the voice of a child who'd just discovered the world was a cruel and lonely place. Cass choked down the shame and pity that rose in her and looked for a way to take advantage of the beast's confusion and distress. She decided to go straight for its heart, the location clearly marked by the pink, embroidered heart that framed its name.

Sorry, Fred, Cass thought as she lowered the point of her sword, aimed at its heart, and ran at the thing like a jousting knight.

Cass, though, was a beat too slow. The monster backhanded her against the wall and her sword clattered to the floor between its legs. It threw back its head and roared at her in anger and pain, sniffling back tears. It lifted a giant foot to squash her before she could get back up, but Cass rolled away just in time. The beast stomped again and again, each time just missing Cass.

Cass, though, was running out of hallway. She struggled to her feet, braced against the back wall.

Then, like a bolt of lightning, the scene before Cass cracked in two as she heard that familiar, violent voice call her name again: "Cassandra!"

It felt to Cass as if, in response to that crack of lightning, time itself had been split down the middle, as if time had forked between two possible paths, two possible worlds, while she, somehow, remained poised between them, undecided. One fork unfolded along a line where, with its next move, the monster pinned her in the corner and crushed her head against the wall. The other fork unfolded along a line where, with her next move, Cass swept the monster's weak leg and sent it crashing backwards, splitting its head like a melon on the axe still embedded in the stone floor.

With a gentle push, Cass chose which line of falling dominoes to set in motion and then, almost as a spectator, watched the events unfold: she swept the leg, the monster toppled backwards, and its head split open. When the sequence ended, Cass found herself thrown abruptly back into time, snapping back into alignment with her own present self, standing victorious over the beast's body as blood and brains drained from its skull.

Aligned again with her own present body, time started flowing smoothly, regularly again. She could hear Zach calling for her, panicked, from the crypt. One moment she had been there in the crypt with him, the next she was, from his perspective, gone. Whatever bubble of time Cass had just been living in, hadn't included him. Atlantis rubbed up against her leg—he'd come back for her—pulling her with his tail toward Zach, the hidden stairs, and the possibility of escape. Cass moved to follow the cat, unsure what had just happened or why.

However, just as she rounded the corner, she heard the violently familiar voice call one last time. "Cassandra," the voice whispered, melancholic.

In response, Atlantis froze, the hair on his back standing on end. He looked like he might run back to the voice.

Cass had had enough.

"We're done," she decided, scooping up Atlantis. Cass took Zach's extended hand and jumped over the side of crypt, onto the stairwell. Together, they took the stairs two at a time, running to catch up with Maya, and Cass didn't look back again.

24

MAYA HADN'T GOTTEN far. But it didn't look like she'd been waiting for them either. They sprinted down the narrow Underside hallway. The passage looked identical to the one that Cass and Zach had initially used: blank walls, a single bare bulb hanging from the ceiling, ninety degree angles framing the turns.

Maya seemed to know where they were going. Cass tried to her empty mind and just run. She emptied her head into her feet and focused on the feel of her rubber soles on the concrete floor as they rolled through each stride. Her pace faltered only once. After their second left turn, she thought she saw, out of the corner of her eye, another locked and unmarked door, flush with the wall. But when she looked back with her good eye, all she saw was an empty wall.

The hallways stretched on until, as before, they were suddenly out in the open, standing under the domed, twilight sky of an Underside hub. Cass bent over, hands on her knees, trying to catch her breath. Zach, hands on his hips, stayed close by her side. Atlantis, without look-ing back, bolted into the crowd and disappeared. Maya, her waist-length hair still impeccably braided, looked like she'd just stepped out of a fashion magazine aiming to sell trendy tactical gear to semi-professional body-builders.

They all waited a beat, eyes fixed on the tunnel's mouth, to see if anything had followed them.

Nothing.

When Cass and Zach turned to go, Maya had al-ready slipped off into the crowd. They couldn't see her head above the mass of people, but they could detect the collateral ripple that signaled her passage. The crowd parted for her like a school of guppies for a shark.

Cass and Zach fought to catch up. The crowd did not part for them.

Cass had a hard time focusing on the work of ma-neuvering through the throng. She was still shaken by her novel experience of forked time. The implications seemed staggering. But, more immediately, she felt a kind of unbearable lightness deep inside her chest, expanding and contracting in time with her still pound-ing heart. She felt transparent, as if, beneath her clothes, she were composed of translucent layers of fine hairs, pale skin, red muscle, blue veins, pink organs, and white bone. She could feel her own skull, pale and cold and empty, bobbing like a balloon tethered to her spine by a string. She felt raw and naked and exposed. She felt incredibly powerful and enormously fragile.

She let go of Zach's hand and stopped for a moment in the middle of the crowd, folding her arms across her chest and squeezing her legs together in an irrational gesture of modesty and vulnerability, afraid that anyone looking would see right through her.

Zach draped his coat over her shoulders and pulled her close, tucking her under his arm. She flinched instinctively but then hung on to him for dear life. He kissed her on the forehead and guided her through the busy streets. Step by step, the sensation drained away and she felt more herself.

Soon, they were back at the York office tower and she was barely trembling.

Maya was already inside the lobby at the security desk, her back to them. She gestured impatiently. The guard pulled something dark off the countertop, stuffed it under the counter, and then handed back her bag. She examined the contents and zipped it up tight.

Zach and Cass pushed through the revolving doors and into the lobby. Even from across the room, Cass could see the guards stiffen at the sight of her, sweat beading on their foreheads. The guards, though, were clearly more afraid of Maya. At a nod from her, they moved to surround Zach and Cass, nightsticks and Tasers drawn.

"What is this," Zach shouted at Maya. He sounded angry and, despite himself, a bit hurt. "What's going on?"

"I am sorry," Maya said calmly, "but our business is done. Know, though, that I am grateful for your help in securing the relic."

Cass's cheeks burned bright red.

"We're not going anywhere," Cass said, watching the guards hesitate in response, "until I've talked to Richard."

Maya shook her head sadly. "I am afraid that is not possible, Cassandra. Richard is *definitely* not here today."

Maya bowed at the waist, more polite than deferential, and turned to go, but stopped and added: "Thanks, too, for the Gospel of St. Paul. In the long run, it will be even more valuable than the chains."

Maya patted her vest pocket where she'd secured the manuscript. For just a moment she looked surprised, then angry. Her eyes narrowed.

"Do you mean this book?" Zach asked, holding up the slim volume.

Maya's eyes narrowed even further. She hefted the bag with the relic, the veins in her forearm popping, her long braid swinging.

"We only need the relic, Maya," Cass said, her voice cracking. "We just need to save Miranda. Let us have the relic and the books is yours."

Maya weighed her options. She looked Zach up and down, but locked eyes with Cass. Her expression softened uncharacteristically, edging toward pity.

"As you wish," Maya said. She put the bag down and, with a graceful kick, sent it sliding across the polished floor.

Cass picked up the bag. Zach handed the manuscript to the nearest guard.

"My advice is to move quickly," Maya said. "You are running out of time."

She looked ready to go but, after a pause, Maya directed one last comment at Cass. "You are so young, Cassandra. You understand so little. I do sincerely hope that, in the end, you do not find what you are looking for. It will destroy you."

With that, Maya disappeared through a side door and Zach and Cass were shuffled back onto the street.

They were hardly out the door, though, before Cass grabbed Zach's hand and started pulling him down the street.

"She's right," Cass said, "we *are* running out of time."

25

THE CROWDED STREETS were beginning to thin. It didn't take them long to get back to BO-BS cantina. Zach hesitated at the door, remembering how he'd been pawed and cornered during their first visit.

"Come on, tough guy," Cass said. "I'll still protect you."

Business had also slowed inside. The tone was subdued, the male dancers off duty, the lights dimmed, and the customers that remained were all gathered in little knots around tables and booths, nursing drinks. However time worked in the Underside, the whole hub seemed to be quieting down.

Once Zach got a look at the now somber room, he stopped trying to hide behind Cass, straightened up, and took the lead. They didn't have any trouble navigating their way toward the back.

They expected to have to get past the bouncer again, but no one was posted at the door. Zach knocked. No response. Cass turned the knob and gave the door a gentle shove, letting it swing open to give them a view of the room. The lights were off and the space was dim.

Cass drew her sword and flicked on the light with the tip of the blade.

The office was empty. The pneumatic tubes that branched wildly along the ceiling, disappearing into the walls, were silent. The whole room had the feel of an empty stage, abandoned as soon as the performance was complete.

"Damn it," Cass whispered.

They took a closer look around the room, trying to keep their growing panic in check. Zach checked the closets and looked behind the door. Cass took a closer look at the desk.

The images and scrollwork carved into the surface of the desk caught her attention. Already, in just over twenty-four hours, a thin layer of dust had collected on the surface. She wiped it clean with her sleeve. The images varied and included a whole menagerie of mythological creatures—unicorns, dragons, phoenixes —but these diverse elements were all tied together by iconography that was explicitly Christian. She traced the larger patterns in the work and noticed that they skillfully led the eye toward a specific focal point: the scrollwork that embedded the reference to "LUKE 15:24."

Cass tapped her finger on the verse. Zach was looking over her shoulder now.

"What is it?" Zach asked.

"Luke 15:24," Cass said, closing her eyes, searching her memory. "It's from Luke's version of the parable of the prodigal son: 'For this my son was dead, and is alive again; he was lost, and is found.'"

"Huh. What about this?" Zach asked again, pointing to an older carving on the margins of the desk. "What's the secret message here?"

In crude letters, it said: FOR A GOOD TIME CALL . . .

Cass shook her head sternly, caught off guard, trying not to laugh.

"I think that might be my old number," Zach added, a hopeful edge to his voice.

He slipped his arms around Cass's waist. She leaned back into him and couldn't stop from laughing now. This time, he didn't try to stop himself from kissing the nape of her neck. Cass surrendered to the distraction, stretched her arms high over her head, and inclined her neck to one side, inviting him to continue. Zach nibbled on her ear, his hands sliding higher on her ribs.

"Sorry to interrupt," Amare said from the doorway, his French inflection more obvious this time. "But a little bird told me that you had returned. I had begun to despair of your success. I fear Miranda may feel the same way."

Cass's arms dropped to her side, one hand itching for her sword.

"The relic is in the bag?" Amare asked. "Hand it over."

"What about the deal?" Zach countered. "You promised us information in return."

"Relic first, information second," Amare said, his hand outstretched.

Zach was reluctant to trust him, especially after what had just happened with Maya. But Cass was tired of delays. She tossed the bag to Amare. He glanced inside and zipped it back up.

"Thank you, Miss Jones," Amare said. "Now, to make good on my end of the bargain, I need to tell you two things."

He held up one finger.

"First, Miranda was, in fact, abducted and is currently being held at a remote location. However, she is not being held by the Lost—though her abductors certainly went out of their way to give that impression."

Cass was out from behind the desk now. Amare had her full attention.

"Miranda is, instead, being held by 'the Shield,' a secret society of magicians who practice the ancient Japanese art of *kotodama* to manipulate reality with words and symbols. They think of themselves as the good guys. They are self-styled defenders of the status quo, and—speaking from personal experience—I assure you that they can be quite ruthless when it comes to dealing with anyone, friend or enemy, who gets in their way."

He extended his free hand with a folded piece of paper between two fingers. Cass took it.

"Miranda is being held at their base in the mountains of Japan. It was originally an ancient monastery. This map will get you there."

"It doesn't matter to me who they are," Cass said as she started for the door, her jaw set and her face grim. "I'll tear them apart."

"Oh, I believe you," Amare said, stepping aside but gently grazing her arm with his hand as she passed by.

Cass stopped in the doorway to see what else he wanted. Zach was still on the far side of the desk. Amare was positioned between them.

"But that was only the *first* thing you needed to know. The second thing may be equally important."

Cass was confident she didn't want to hear whatever was going to come next.

"You should also know that your boyfriend, Zach Riviera, is one of the Shield's top agents."

26

MIRANDA WAS CHAINED to a wall in what could fairly be described as a "dungeon." The room was cold, the stone walls and stone floor had chilled her to the bone. Her wrists were red and raw. Her arms ached from being suspended from the wall above her head. Her emotions bounced between anger, pity, and despair. But regardless of how she felt, the focal point of her emotions was the same: Kumiko.

Keys turned and the bolt in the heavy lock on her cell door clunked free. A moment later, the door to her cell banged open. Pushed too hard, it rebounded off the wall. An enormous figure ducked his head and, leading with his shoulder, squeezed his bulk through the door. His ridiculously large hands stilled the door. The fading evening light cast stark shadows across his face, highlighting the fact that his cheeks were pitted with deep acne scars.

"Hello, Dogen," Miranda said weakly. She rolled her eyes upward, taking him in without lifting her head. He looked identical to how he'd looked when she'd met him thirty years ago: looming and gentle and ponytailed. "I think it's time to consider a haircut. Even in the mountains of Japan, the '90s are long gone."

Dogen stopped short, his hand smoothing his hair, seriously considering her advice.

Kumiko stepped out of the shadows behind him. She looked like a child next to Dogen. "There's no reason to be cruel," she said. "We're all just doing whatever must be done." Her hands were clasped in front of her, hidden in the sleeves of her kimono. Her white hair was gathered in a tight bun.

Kumiko continued. "Clearly *you* were just doing what you felt must be done. Even if that meant betraying the Shield. Even if that meant betraying me."

Miranda let her head hang, eyes down, her weight suspended from the chains that bound her wrists.

"You're wrong," Miranda whispered.

"I wish that were true," Kumiko replied, her voice cold and reserved. She paused, and softened slightly. "I *do* wish it were true. But you've always put your own family first. Your loyalties have never really been to us."

Kumiko gestured to Dogen. He dragged an old stool from the corner of the room and set it closer to Miranda. Kumiko sat down, her feet barely touching the floor. Dogen then brought a bucket of water with a metal ladle in from the hall and set it where Miranda could see it. It looked like ordinary water but, trained in *kotodama*, Miranda knew that the glimmering water's green tint indicated something more: "interrogation water."

Infused with a spell, the water would wear away her mental defenses, making her cooperative and her responses truthful.

Dogen ladled a scoop of the water over her head. The water was freezing cold and Miranda winced and wilted in response, shrinking back into herself. The tiny ladle, though, was unwieldy in Dogen's massive hands and, returning it to the bucket, he splashed some water on himself.

Kumiko shot him a disapproving look. Dogen looked away, abashed. Miranda couldn't say for sure, but she thought that he now looked even more cooperative and compliant than normal. He looked like he was ready to spill all his secrets.

"You have recklessly endangered us all," Kumiko said, returning to both her monologue and her icy demeanor. "Without authorization or consultation you revealed yourself to Cassandra and involved yourself in a maverick, globe-trotting adventure that resulted in the death of Judas and the catastrophic destabilization of the fragile balance between the Lost, the Turned, and the ordinary world—a balance that we had worked so hard, for so long, to ensure."

Kumiko rose to her feet and, despite her height, she towered over Miranda.

"You were a faithful disciple for so many years. You had such promise, even after what happened with your sister. But I should have seen what was coming. In the end, like your sister, you were incapable of patience. You leap into action and gamble everything without weighing the consequences of your actions or foreseeing their ramifications."

Miranda felt a flicker of anger when Kumiko mentioned Rose but, soaked in interrogation water, she had no fuel to burn.

"I know that you were looking for the new leader of the Lost, the one they call the Heretic, and that you had reached out to them without authorization and were pursuing sources outside Shield protocol. And I know, too, that in a foolish effort to save you from your own people"—Miranda looked up at this, an honestly skeptical look in her eyes at the mention of the Shield being "her own people"—"Cassandra has, once again, enlisted help from the Turned, secured a valuable relic, and then willingly handed that relic over to the Lost themselves."

This last revelation hit Miranda hard. "Oh, Cass," she said softly to herself, shaking her head. "Not for me."

"Your girl is a one-man wrecking crew," Kumiko said, raising her voice. "If her emotions break loose, she may single handedly destroy the world itself before the week is out!"

Kumiko almost shouted this last bit, her frustration wearing through. Pacing the length of the cell, she smoothed her kimono, calming herself.

"You have failed Miranda. Your whole family has failed. And Cassandra won't be able to help you now. She may find her way here, but when she does, she'll just be stepping into a trap. And once we also have her in hand, we may finally be able to start cleaning up this mess you have made."

Dogen was getting a little antsy, shifting his weight back and forth from one foot to the other, primed as he was by the water to be extra cooperative and compliant. He looked like he might jump in and start helpfully answering questions *for* Miranda.

"I need to know the truth," Kumiko continued, lifting Miranda's chin to look her in the eye. "I need to know what you know. I need to know: who is the new leader of the Lost?"

Miranda looked right back as her mixed emotional response to Kumiko finally resolved itself, moving from the spark of anger to an abiding sense of pity.

Miranda pitied her.

Kumiko would never be able to see the truth—she was too frozen to thaw to its warmth. And whatever bond of trust and friendship had once existed between them was gone now, irreparably broken.

Miranda gathered herself together, drawing herself up to her full height.

"I'll tell you what I know," Miranda said. "I'll tell you the thing you've been hiding from yourself for centuries. I'll tell you the thing that you're most afraid to hear."

Kumiko took a step back. Dogen moved to her side.

"I'll tell you the truth," Miranda finished, "about the Lost."

27

SILENCE. THE WHOLE trip back to Cass's apartment, neither of them spoke. Cass might have left Zach behind if she had been sure she could get back by herself. But she wasn't. So she stuck with him, staying a few steps behind, the sense of hopelessness that had dogged her for months—always two frustrating steps removed, never quite felt in the first person—souring now into a sense of betrayal. With every step, this sense of betrayal gathered steam until, back in the apartment, Cass couldn't hold it in any longer.

Cass dropped her gear in the corner and wheeled on Zach, her finger already pointed at him, her weak eye wandering. The sun was down and the apartment windows were black.

Zach took a couple of steps back, his hands raised defensively.

"I know it's true," Cass said. "I know Amare was telling the truth—about the Shield and about you." She felt in her pocket for the reassuring square of paper that contained the map leading to Miranda's location. It was still there.

Zach didn't try to deny it.

Cass kept advancing and Zach kept retreating. Without quite meaning to, Zach ended up circling behind the Wing Chun practice dummy, positioning it between the two of them.

Cass's hand closed into a fist. She unleashed her frustration on the practice dummy, delivering a couple of blows that rattled the worn wooden arms in their sockets.

"You work for the Shield?" Cass asked again, giving him a chance to confess.

"Yes," Zach admitted. "I have for a long time. They recruited me when I was barely a teen and they trained me for years. They keep an eye out for kids that show some sensitivity to magic. It's how I got involved in all this in the first place."

"And Miranda?" Cass asked.

"Yes, Miranda worked with the Shield, too," Zach confirmed. "I knew about her by reputation, but our paths never crossed until after I met you."

"Why would they kidnap one of their own people? It doesn't make any sense," Cass pressed, rocking the dummy in its stand with a kick.

Zach looked at the dummy, still rocking, and back at Cass.

"Miranda had . . . a reputation. She was a bit of a wild card and her relationship with her bosses at the Shield had been strained for a long time. The details aren't clear to me. But when, last year, she got sucked into that confrontation with Judas, everything went to hell. Nobody trusted her anymore and they ordered me to keep an eye on her and what she was doing. When she went looking for the new leader of the Lost on her own, they must have decided that they had to intervene and bring her back in—whether she wanted to come in or not."

Cass chewed on her lip, trying to process this. She circled around the dummy toward Zach, but he kept circling, too, keeping some space between them.

He guessed what her next question was going to be and tried to beat her to it.

"I didn't know, Cass," he said. "I didn't know *why* they wanted me to keep an eye on her. And I didn't know until Amare said it that the Shield, not the Lost, really did have her."

He looked at his shoes and then back up at her.

"You've got to believe me."

Cass believed him. But now that gears had been set in motion, all of the wheels in her mind were turning. Everything that had happened in the past year took on a different shape. In fact, everything in the past twenty years started to take on a different shape. And all of these wheels within wheels seemed to turn in connection with the mystery she understood least: what had happened to her mother. In one way or another, her mother had been entangled in all of this.

Cass felt the fight drain out of her at the thought of how little she understood. She wandered toward a stool and was about to sit down when an additional thought struck her with the force of revelation: her friendship with Zach was no coincidence.

Her blood flushed hot again and she was back on our feet, fists balled.

"They asked you to watch Miranda," Cass asked, "because you were already here."

"Yeah," Zach said, "but I didn't like the idea."

"Fine. But why were you *already* here?"

Zach looked like Cass had just punched him in the gut, his face a shade of green.

"Why, Zach? Why were you already here? We didn't meet by accident did we? Our friendship is no coincidence, is it? They assigned you to 'watch' me, too, didn't they? They assigned you to be my 'friend'?"

Zach didn't even have to answer. She knew it was true.

Zach started to offer some kind of explanation. Cass cut him off.

Everything that came next landed with a dull thud of inevitability. Everything that came next couldn't *not* be said.

"Was it part of your job to get me to fall in love with you, too? Friendship wasn't enough?"

Zach stopped retreating. Cass caught up to him and punched him in the shoulder.

"Did your bosses order you to get into my pants, too? Did they train you, like some fucking super-spy, to seduce me? Or did you improvise that part of the plan on your own?"

She punched him again, hard, in the same shoulder, then kicked the couch and sent it sliding across the floor.

He stayed silent, head bowed, holding his ground, and took it.

"Asshole," Cass spat. "Fuck you. It's time to pick a side. It's time to decide if you're on my side or theirs."

Zach swallowed hard.

"Are you going to help me rescue Miranda, or not?"

Zach hesitated. "It's not that simple, Cass. I need some time. Give me just a little bit of time to try and sort this out, to see what is really going on, before we rush in there, guns blazing."

That sounded sensible, but it also felt like a dodge.

"Are you sure that Miranda has that time to spare?"

Zach didn't know what to say.

"I gave you a choice," Cass said quietly. "It looks like you've made yours. Get out."

Cass locked the door behind him.

28

CASS PACED THE length of her apartment like a caged tiger. Save for some light from the street, the room was dark. Her emotions rattled against their cages. She felt torn between her feelings for Zach and her sense of betrayal. Even though they weren't really a couple and there was no other woman, it *felt* liked he'd been cheating on her for years. She was glad he was gone.

No, that wasn't true. And she couldn't afford to let her head spin lies right now. The truth was, she was terrified: terrified that his departure meant the only real thing she thought she knew and understood in her life —Zach—was gone forever. She felt her breath catch as her chest tightened to the point of physical pain at the thought.

Her anger at his betrayal flared, resisting even the slightest hint of forgiveness. And she wasn't forgiving him.

All she knew was that her powers had done nothing but affirm the truth of Zach's own feelings for her.

Which meant there were pieces in play that she didn't understand. The pain in her chest returned.

Clearly, this line of thought wasn't helping. She tried to push through that fog and focus on Miranda.

She stopped in front of her desk, switched on the desk lamp, and cleared away the piles of books, research, and writing that had gone into her doctoral dissertation. She put a couple stacks on the floor and just pushed others to the edge. She'd hardly touched these things in months and, once she had a space cleared, she wiped away the thin layer of dust that had accumulated with the back of her hand. She stared at the grain of the wood as if she'd just wiped the steam from a bathroom mirror and expected an image to appear. But nothing did.

Cass pulled the square of paper from her pocket— the map that Amare had given her—and spread it out on the desk. She leaned over the image and instructions, both arms braced against the desk. Her arms were thin but roped with muscle. It was a map of the Underside and it sketched an abridged path through hallways and hubs from her apartment to the Shield base in Japan. She guessed it wouldn't take more than an hour to get there.

She shook her head in disbelief. An hour of walking. To Japan. A few days ago she wouldn't have believed it.

The world was *not* what she'd always thought it was.

This thought hit her hard, disorienting her. She felt dizzy and lightheaded and sat down hard in the chair that she'd pushed aside, almost missing the seat. She leaned forward into the small circle of light created by her desk lamp and squeezed her head between the palms of her hands.

"You can do this, Jones," she said to herself out loud. "You can do this."

But she wasn't sure she could. Getting there wouldn't be simple but it wouldn't be the hard part either. Before, at the warehouse, she's gotten just a small taste of what she would face at the Shield base. Did she really think she could sneak in, snag Miranda, and handle whatever opposition she would face along the way? One false step and she'd bring the whole base down on herself.

Cass looked up at the map, her vision blurred now by tears. She felt the tears run down her face as if they belonged to someone else. The map was clear but the job seemed impossible.

With the heels of her hands, Cass wiped her eyes. The corner of an old framed photo poking out from the back of her desk behind piles of books caught her attention.

She pulled it free and took a closer look. It was a photo of Cass, Rose, and Miranda. They were all scrunched together on a couch in Cass's childhood home. Cass was nine, Miranda was holding a glass of wine, and Rose was smiling and squeezing Cass.

Cass couldn't just let Miranda go. She couldn't just go back to work tomorrow and pretend that everything was fine. Even if she was likely to fail in any attempt to rescue her, she had to try. Time wasn't going to fork on this occasion. There was no second path.

Cass pulled on some warmer clothes and grabbed her sword. She folded the map and tucked it back into her pocket.

Cass pulled a cushion of the couch, ready to step inside and head down the stairs, but the couch was just a couch. All she found inside was dust bunnies and spare change.

"Come on!" Cass mumbled to herself.

She put the cushion back and stepped back. The couch wasn't in its usual spot. She'd kicked it when Zach was still here. She pushed it back to its normal location and pulled the cushion off again. A yawning void and narrow flight of stairs opened up in front of her.

Cass stepped into the couch and squeezed down the stairs. At the bottom, she found the narrow hallway with the single bare bulb that she'd expected. She consulted her map. Two lefts and then a right.

Halfway down that first hallway, Cass passed the unmarked door, locked and flush against the wall. She hesitated for just a moment, then pushed forward. She hadn't gone more than a couple of steps, though, before she was brought up short: someone or something was pounding on the door from the inside. The blows were loud and powerful.

Cass hesitated again—for just a moment—then took off running down the hallway.

29

CASS EMERGED FROM the Underside tunnel to find herself at the mouth of a cave, high in mountains of Japan. Snow covered the ground. Her breath steamed in the frigid mountain air.

The night sky was clear and, far from any city lights, the stars shone close and deep and bright. Cass shivered —partly from the cold, and partly from the intense, cosmic sense of loneliness and disorientation induced by the magnitude of the sky. She felt dizzy. She felt like she was floating upward, like she was in danger of being swallowed whole by the icy void that yawned open above her head as the sky vaulted, unbroken, from horizon to horizon.

She leaned over, hands on her knees, and looked down. Breathing deeply, she tried to reconnect with the solid earth beneath her feet. When her head finally stopped spinning, she looked out over the valley below. She found herself at the edge of the forest, positioned on an outcropping that overlooked the scene.

She had a clear look at the layout of the monastery compound and she could observe, without danger of being seen, the movements of the guards as they cycled through their shifts and patrol routes. Amare had known what he was doing when he'd had her exit here. It was just what she needed.

The compound was walled. Its interior contained a complex of buildings arranged around a central courtyard and the courtyard itself was centered on what appeared to be a well. Cass didn't have any trouble identifying the building where Miranda was being held. Closest to the base of the mountain, one building was different from the others. This building, clearly older and larger than the rest, presided over the compound with an air of ancient, monastic authority. Amare's map indicated that Cass would find Miranda in the basement.

Cass watched, still and silent, for a full hour until she was confident that she knew what the guard rotations looked like and had decided how she planned to slip their defenses. When she finally took action and started down through the remaining stand of trees and into the valley, her cold, stiff, tired muscles protested. Cass, though, welcomed the burn in her thighs and she was grateful that the work of slipping soundlessly through the trees required her full attention. The flaring pain, combined with the demanding terrain, helped her to ignore the riot of emotions in her own heart and head.

Her emotions felt as dangerously close to the surface as they'd felt in a long time.

Now, though, was not the time to get back in touch with herself. Her emotions wouldn't help her, they'd overrun her. The key was to stay focused on what she needed to do to get Miranda out. And, above all, the key was to make sure that she didn't let herself think about Zach. She couldn't let herself get lost in the fog of anger and betrayal that accompanied every thought of him.

Keep going, Cass. One foot in front of the other. Feel the burn. Absorb the terrain.

Before she knew it, she arrived at the bottom of the slope. The compound's western wall extended almost to the stand of trees. She waited in the shadows of the forest. If she'd timed it right, the next pair of guards should pass by any minute now.

The pair of guards emerged into view. Both were young and both were about Cass's height. They were exactly the kind of B-grade, undersized trainees likely to get late night guard duty along the perimeter. They were huddled together against the chill of the wind that howled down the length of the compound wall. They were having an animated conversation—Cass couldn't quite hear at first—about Cass.

"We've got to stay alert," the shorter one said to the other. "Dogen will have our heads if Jones slips by us."

"I'm not half as worried about Dogen as I am about Kumiko," said the other. "Kumiko wouldn't stop with having our heads."

They both nodded in agreement.

"I've heard stories about her," the second one continued, "about Jones. They say she's a Seer. They say that even Kumiko is afraid of her."

The shorter guard agreed again.

Encouraged, the other continued. "I've heard that she's legendary with a sword, that her blade moves so fast it only appears as a flash of light."

Cass, in the shadows, drew her sword in anticipation of their approach. She made sure it didn't reflect any glint of light from the compound. The guards were getting close now.

"I've also heard that she's more than six feet tall," he said, gesturing with one hand raised above his head, indicating Cass's expected height.

Cass shifted her weight from one foot to the other, drawing herself up to her full height of barely five feet, poised for action.

"Yeah, that's true. And also I've heard that she's got long blond hair and enormous breasts," the first chimed in, a hopeful note to his voice, miming with both hands the expected dimensions of Cass's—apparently—very svelte figure.

Cass checked that her shoulder length, black hair was still pulled tight in its pony tail. Then, despite herself, she glanced down at her slim, athletic chest. She thought it over for a moment, then shrugged.

"Yes, yes," the other replied, "I've heard the same. She's an American after all and all American women are blond with big breasts. I've seen the videos. And, more than that, I've heard that just one look at her can freeze a man in place. Men are mesmerized by her beauty and then, frozen in place, they are powerless to move as she effortlessly cuts them down with her sword." He mimed the stroke of a sword, decapitating his companion. His companion played along, eyes wide with some combination of desire and horror at the imagined sight of Cass.

They were both nodding eagerly now, their heads bobbing in time together.

They were almost on top off her. Wraithlike, Cass stepped out from behind a tree, sword raised, onto the path directly in front of them.

Both guards immediately froze in place, scanning her from head to toe, trying in vain to make what they'd just imagined fit the reality of what they were seeing.

"I guess I'm even more beautiful than you dared imagine," Cass said drily as she delivered a roundhouse kick to the head of one and a blow with the hilt of her sword to the chin of the other.

Both men crumpled to the ground. Cass searched them for keys, gagged them, and then tied them, unconscious, to a tree out of sight from the path.

As soon as they were bundled away and she had what she needed, Cass was surprised to find that she missed their banter. If she could manage to be half of what they feared, she might actually have a shot at rescuing Miranda.

Cass slipped through a gate and along the interior of the wall. Another pair of guards, more serious and less chatty, passed by her hiding spot, oblivious. Their spears cast long shadows in the low angled light of the nearest fire burning in the courtyard.

Cass stuck close to Amare's instructions. She circled around the back of the main building and located a ground-level window. The latch was loose and, just as two more guards turned the corner, dropped into a basement hallway. Staying low to the ground and close to the wall, she wound her way down one hallway, took a left, and down another. The deeper she went in the building, the older everything seemed. Concrete floors gave way to stone. Metal doors gave way to wood.

Peeking around the corner of Miranda's hallway, Cass saw just one guard stationed next to the door. She fished along the seams of the uneven floor for a loose stone and found one about the size of a dime. She tossed it around the corner, low to the ground. It landed on the far side of the guard, drawing his attention. The moment his head was turned, Cass took a run at him. In full stride, just as his head was swiveling back in her direction, Cass leapt and unleashed a vicious punch, aided by gravity and the full weight of her body. The guard slumped to the ground, unconscious.

Cass sucked on her knuckle, split and bleeding from the force of the blow, and took stock of the heavy wooden door, hung on ancient iron hinges, that barred entrance to Miranda's cell. The massive iron bolt that locked it in place required no key. It only required that you not be inside the cell.

Cass took a deep breath. Now that she was here, she was afraid to open it.

30

CASS HESITATED. SHE wasn't sure what she would find on the other side of the door. Would Miranda be alive? Would she be wounded? Would she still be Miranda? What if Miranda had betrayed the Shield and was, in some way, in league with the Lost? What would Cass do then?

She didn't know. But there was only one way to find out.

Cass slid back the bolt and leaned her full weight against the door. It creaked open a few inches, just enough for Cass to squeeze inside.

It took a moment for her eyes to adjust to darkness. When they did, Cass found Miranda where Kumiko had left her: chained to the wall, wet and freezing, the weight of her body borne by her bruised and raw wrists.

"Miranda," Cass whispered, trying to get her attention. "Miranda, it's me. Cass."

Miranda's head lolled to the side, her eyes pointed in Cass's general direction, but she didn't reply.

"I'm here to . . . rescue you," Cass said, feeling ridiculous even as she said it. She put her arms around Miranda, helping her stand on her own two feet, relieving the weight from her wrists. Miranda let out a deep sigh as if she had been holding her breath all this time. Her skin was pale and ice cold. Cass leaned in and kissed her on the forehead.

"I'm so sorry, Miranda," Cass said. "Let's get you out of here."

In response, Miranda mumbled a few broken phrases that Cass could only partly make out. "Go, Cass . . . get out . . . leave me . . . Kumiko is coming . . . she . . . a trap."

"Just hang in there, Miranda," Cass said, aiming for a tone that sounded confident and reassuring.

Cass leveraged her sword in the clasps of Miranda's manacles and, one after the other, popped them open. Freed, Miranda wilted and collapsed to the ground. Cass slid her hands under Miranda's head just before it would have hit the stone floor. She removed her jacket, slipped Miranda into it, and pulled her into her lap. She rubbed Miranda's arms and legs, trying to generate some warmth and bring her back around.

Miranda's eyes opened a crack. She recognized Cass immediately but it wasn't clear if she understood where they were or what was happening.

"Cass," Miranda tried again, her blue lips cracked, her left eye bruised. "I should have told you."

Her voice faltered but, before Cass could interrupt, she tried again. "All the flowers, all the blossoms, all the roses and tulips and petals and thorns . . . I had to find out if it was true . . . but I should have told you, I should have trusted you . . . but I was afraid I was wrong . . . so many flowers . . . I had to find out what was happening with the Lost . . ."

Miranda's eyes lost focus and she trailed off. Cass didn't know what to make of that string of riddles. But she did know they had to get out of there. And the longer they delayed, the poorer their chances would become.

Cass swung Miranda's arm over her own shoulder and, with a grunt, stood, bringing them both to their feet. She bore most of Miranda's weight as they shuffled toward the door and out into the hall. The guard was still unconscious next to the door and Cass didn't hear the sounds of anyone approaching.

"The flowers, Cass," Miranda continued to mumble. "I had to see."

"Shhhh, Miranda," Cass whispered. "Just be quiet now and work with me."

Miranda's bone-white feet found some footing and her weak knees bore a bit more of her weight. Following Cass's lead, they worked their way down the hall, around the corner, and up a flight of stairs. There was no way they could exit through the window Cass had used to enter.

They didn't encounter anyone. The building had the mute feel of something abandoned.

Cass had been terrified they would bump into someone and the alarm would sound. Now, she was beginning to worry because they *hadn't* bumped into anyone yet. Where was everyone?

They exited the stairwell on the first floor. With her sword in one hand and Miranda supported with the other, Cass shunted them out a side door and into an alley between two buildings. Cass could hear a pair of guards rounding the perimeter and, without any real choice, found herself flushed out of the alley and into the compound's courtyard.

As soon as they stepped out into the courtyard, a series of floodlights lit up the space as bright as noonday. A phalanx of guards emerged from hiding and surrounded them. At the head of the party, near the well, was the giant of a man that Cass had barely escaped in the warehouse.

In response to the light, Miranda looked up. "Dogen," she murmured.

Cass was frozen like a deer in headlights, the sinking feeling in the pit of her stomach pinning her in place. There was no way she could fight them all. There was no way she could protect Miranda while she tried. There was no way that, together, they could manage to escape.

"Shit," Cass said in response. "Shit, shit, *shit.*"

The guards encircling them didn't move. They stood frozen in place, waiting for something—or someone.

A rumble passed through the crowd as Dogen stepped to the side and, out of his shadow, a tiny woman in a kimono joined the circle. She advanced toward Cass and Miranda and the circle closed behind her. Cass knew her wrinkled face and white hair immediately. It was the woman from her memory of the cherry blossom festival, the woman whose presence her father had lied about.

"Kumiko," Miranda said.

"Kumiko," Cass repeated to herself, recognizing as she said it that the name fit like a glove.

The old woman stood at a distance, her arms folded inside the sleeves of her kimono, appraising them.

"You look so much like your mother," Kumiko offered. "I'm sorry that the two of you aren't *less* like her in the end."

Kumiko drew her hands out from her sleeves and, chanting quietly in Japanese, began to weave threads of green light together, her hands dancing in time with the rhythm of the song. The threads of green light intertwined and extended toward Cass and Miranda, enveloping them.

The net began to constrict around them. Cass took a swing with her sword but the blow had no effect. Before she could try again, the shimmering green web cinched tight, pinning her arms to her side.

Cass felt the will to fight drain out of her. Her knees buckled, her sword fell from her hand, and her vision went black around the edges. The spell didn't just constrain her physically, it dampened her will and slowed her mind to molasses.

Just as she was about to lose hold of the world, she saw Dogen swoop in from the side. He caught her, deftly and gently, cradling her in the palms of his enormous, soft hands.

31

AMARE WAS ONE of the few people who had unfettered access to the Heretic—to the woman who, since the death of Judas, had largely seized control of the Lost.

He'd been working closely with her for many years now, all through the time that Judas, fearful of her, had sent her into exile. He owed her everything. His loyalty was absolute. He loved her.

Amare passed through layers of security, weaving his way deeper into the old but still operating casino in Reno, Nevada, that they had recently co-opted as their new headquarters. The security was meant not only to protect them from outsiders but to protect them, too, from themselves. Many of their number were on the brink of going feral.

Almost four in the morning now, things were winding down on the casino floor. The site was a good fit for them: it offered a viable front for their activities and it was located at a site that, unknown to the former owners, overlapped significantly with the Underside. They could come and go as they pleased without ever being seen.

Amare found his master deep in the casino's command center. The room was full of surveillance feeds from every part of the building. More, the command center connected directly to the casino's vault—a vault that, to a significant degree, his master had repurposed. Now, in addition to handling the normal forms of wealth that flowed through a casino, a portion of the vault was used for storing relics.

As he approached her, Amare hefted the bag containing the relic recovered by Cass. He smiled, reassured by the weight of the chains in the bag. They needed this relic. He hoped that she would be pleased.

"Amare," she said, taking him in. "You're back. You were successful?"

"Yes, master," Amare replied. "Cassandra did as you asked and we passed along the information about Miranda. Kumiko will surely be waiting for her, but I think you're right to wager that, in the process, Kumiko is going to get much more than she bargained for and that, in the end, Cassandra will be disillusioned with them."

She turned her back on the control room and paced into the dimly lit vault. Amare followed her. Given the relics that it contained, the vault felt more like a crypt than a bank.

With an iron thud, Amare set the bag on a table in the center of the room. Almost half of the room was commanded by the wealth of relics that Judas had accumulated over the years and that they had, with exception of the fragments of the One True Cross, recovered from the ruins of his castle. Many of the most powerful relics were displayed and preserved in museum-grade glass cases.

Still with her back to Amare, the Heretic wandered through the vault, tapping her fingernail on each glass case as she walked by.

"Damn these relics," she hissed. "I hate them. I hate the fact that we need them. I hate the fact that, like dumb idols, their power doesn't derive from the truth of what they are but from the masses of ignorant and petty believers who invested them with power."

Amare trailed along behind her, hands clasped behind his back, nodding his head in agreement.

She stopped at a case that displayed the half rotten, half preserved finger of some unlikely saint. It glowed faintly under the warm light positioned above it.

"But the Lost grow *more* lost and feral by the day, Amare," she continued. "They are overrun by their appetites and passions and the only thing preventing them devolving wholly into animals is the power that we draw from these relics. That power is the only thing still binding them with a thin thread of loyalty to us and their own humanity. If that power gives out, if that thread breaks, then they are as likely to destroy us as anyone else. They will rage across the globe, setting in motion a cataclysm the likes of which the world has never seen."

As she spoke, she passed cases containing a golden crown from India and a bejeweled dagger from China, again tapping each glass case with the tip of her fingernail. She stopped in front of a glass case that contained an extraordinarily powerful relic from Alabama: a rabbit's foot, dyed neon pink, suspended from a keychain that said "Suck Balls or Die."

Amare raised an eyebrow. He'd never seen this one before.

"We've got to hang on, Amare. We've got to hang on regardless of the cost. These relics are just stop-gaps. But we are very close—as close as we've ever been—to unlocking the deeper secret we've been looking for."

She circled back around now to the bag on the center table and unzipped it. She removed the heavy chains and laid them out on the table's polished steel surface.

She held her hand out above them, as if she expected them to be hot, as if she were feeling for whatever heat was radiating from them.

But she couldn't sense anything. They were stone cold. These chains were powerless.

Amare retreated when her saw her face go blank and her eyes glow an angry, feral red. Whatever anger was swelling inside of her had breached the dams that, with the help of these relics, she'd set in place inside of herself. Her own appearance slid from the human and toward the animal. Her teeth grew visibly sharper. With one arm, she tore the table from the steel brackets that bolted it to the floor and tossed it across the room, smashing it against the wall.

"They're fakes," Amare said. "We've been played."

"Yes," she confirmed, "but not by Cassandra."

The Heretic turned her back to Amare, struggling to control herself and reassert her humanity.

"Damn you, Richard York," she said to herself. "Damn you and your Turned."

32

CASS WAS CHAINED to the wall, her arms suspended over her head, the tips of her toes just barely touching the floor. Her wrists already felt raw from intermittently bearing her body's full weight. Her hair hung loose around her bowed head. Her vision was still fuzzy and her will still weak from the spell. Trying to think clearly felt like slogging through mud. The room was freezing and they'd taken her socks, shoes, coat, and outer layers of clothing.

Cass wasn't sure how much time had passed. They'd gone to deal with Miranda first, but they would surely be back for her soon.

You're in deep trouble, now, she thought to herself as she struggled to lift her head and get a look around the room.

The cell basically looked like Miranda's. Stone walls and stone floor. A heavy wooden door bolted from the outside. The same iron chains anchoring her to a fat iron ring embedded in the wall above her head. No

window. What she could see of the room was illuminated by the little bit of light that shone from the hallway
through the barred window in the top half of the door.

Cass started to cough and couldn't stop. The coughs
racked her whole body, rattling her chains. She coughed
until it felt like something dark and organic had come
loose inside of her. She spat it out onto the floor. The
residue dripped from her chin like a string of shiny
black pearls.

She felt a little better. Her thoughts seemed to co-
here more readily and her will seemed stronger.

With a clearer head, she took a second look around
the room and, this time, noticed something new. There
was a difference between this cell and Miranda's: in
addition to the heavy wooden door that led to the hall,
there was, in the opposite wall, a second door. The door
was flush with the wall and lacked a handle. It seemed
older than the rest of the already ancient room. It gave
the impossible impression that, somehow, it predated
the construction of the monastery itself, like it had been
standing there long before anyone had bothered to
block in walls around it.

Cass shook her head, trying to clear her vision.
Maybe she wasn't thinking as clearly as she'd thought.
Who knew what residual effects Kumiko's spell might
have.

At the thought of Kumiko, Cass flashed on her
memory of the cherry blossoms. In her mind's eye, Cass
could see Kumiko plainly, framed by the explosion of
pink and white flowers. Kumiko's hand gripped Rose's

upper arm as she leaned over and whispered something in her ear. Rose nodded and smiled in response.

Cass couldn't make sense of it. Had her mother been wrong to trust Kumiko? Had Miranda been wrong to trust Kumiko? Had her father been *right* to lock this all away and hide it from her? Had he been right to pretend that Kumiko didn't even exist?

Cass hung her head.

What was she doing here? What did she *actually* know? Who did she think she was, trying to rescue Miranda on her own, jumping into the middle of something that she barely understood?

The doubts and questions snowballed. For Cass, it felt like the echo of that memory of Kumiko had set in motion an avalanche of emotions that were rushing down the face of time to sweep her away and bury her forever.

Cass couldn't do it anymore. Whatever doors or dams or protective measures had been set in place in her mind to protect her from the force of her emotions —they were failing. Hopelessness broke loose, caught up with her, and overwhelmed her.

Now, for the first time in decades, Cass was *feeling* her own emotions, in the first person, immediately. She was feeling them as her own emotions. And though she greeted their return with a sense of relief, she also felt like she was drowning inside her own mind.

In short, she could feel again, but what she was feeling felt like dying.

The stronger the echo of that memory grew, the deeper Cass felt buried: Kumiko whispering in her mother's ear, Kumiko whispering in her mother's ear, Kumiko whispering in her mother's ear . . . until, subtly, the weight of the memory began to shift from front to back and—instead of it being a memory about Kumiko —it became a memory about her mother.

Kumiko whispering in *her mother's* ear.

Once it became a memory about her mother, the scene stopped looping and the rest of the memory unfolded. Cass found herself in the memory again: she was seven years old and lost in the trees. The shadow loomed over her, enveloping her. Her mother found her and saved her. Her mother told her to repeat a word three times and, while she was saying it, to think of her.

What was the word?

The memory slowed to a crawl and Cass could see her mother's face, her lips forming the word, her breath warm on Cass's cheek.

Kibo.

Her mother's eyes twinkled green and she squeezed Cass's hand and Cass held on to her for dear life and shouted—out loud or just in her own mind, she could no longer tell—*kibo, kibo, kibo!*

In response, the whole of Cass's world contracted to a single black point, like the universe had been rewound to the moment before the big bang, and then it exploded again and Cass was filled with light and she was back in the dungeon and, with a shrug, she casually broke the chains that bound her to the wall.

But, just as abruptly, the light was gone and Cass was herself again. The room was dark. Cass was on her knees. The manacles were still attached to her wrists but they were no longer attached to the chains. Bits and pieces of the heavy iron chains lay scattered on the floor around her.

Cass put her hands on the cold stone floor, trying to catch her breath and process what had just happened.

She could still feel the weight of her hopelessness, immediate and intense and first person, bearing down on her. But something else was different now.

Something else had changed.

She sat back on her heels, swept her hair from her eyes, and saw what it was. The unmarked door on the far side of the room was open.

33

"Meow," the open door said.

An orange tabby cat padded out of the darkness framed by the door. Filled with a deep sense of gratitude and relief, Cass wept as Atlantis jumped into her lap.

She wasn't alone.

"Meow," Atlantis said again as Cass squeezed him tight.

Though her legs were weak and shaking from the force of what she'd experienced, Cass willed herself to stand up and take a couple of uncertain steps toward the open door. With Atlantis still tucked in the crook of one arm, she leaned against the doorframe for support, staring into the ink-black darkness on the far side.

She didn't like what she saw. The darkness seemed alive. It seemed to breathe. Cass stretched out her hand and extended it into the darkness. It felt hot and liquid and primal. She withdrew her hand, expecting to find the darkness still clinging stickily to it, but saw only her own hand.

A wave of vertigo crashed over Cass. Instinctively, she dropped Atlantis and grabbed the doorjamb with both hands, hanging on tight as the room wobbled around her. Cass squeezed her eyes shut and took a deep breath. When the rocking stopped, she opened her eyes again. The room was still.

But the very act of opening her eyes—as if she had been asleep—prompted an unwelcome thought: was she dreaming? Were Atlantis and the door and the darkness just a dream?

Cass touched the darkness again, this time with just the tip of her finger, and it reacted to her touch. Concentric circles rippled outward from the point of contact. This was weird, no doubt, but it didn't feel like a dream.

It felt real.

Still, though she didn't think she was dreaming, "dream" wasn't a bad shorthand for *part* of what was happening. With a start, Cass realized what the darkness really did feel like: it felt like *mind*.

Atlantis curled between her legs, purring reassuringly, and then, like he was responding to a call, dashed through the door and into the darkness, leaving Cass behind.

The Underside, Zach had said, was allied with mind.

Right, Cass thought, *let's take a trip, led by my super-weird cat, into the underside of my mind. Why not? I don't have anything else planned for today.*

Cass swallowed hard and stepped into the inky darkness.

On the far side of the darkness, Cass found a narrow set of stairs that funneled into a bland hallway with a single bare bulb hanging from the ceiling. She walked the full length of the hallway. It came to a dead end.

Where the hell did my cat go? Cass wondered for the thousandth time in her life, staring at the blank wall in front of her and running her hands through hair.

She turned back and retraced her steps, taking a more careful look. Before long she found a side door that she must have missed the first time—or maybe it hadn't been there the first time? It was hard to believe that she would have walked right past it. The door looked just like the other she'd seen: flush with the wall, missing a handle, and fitted with a lock that was ice cold to the touch.

Cass wasn't sure what to do next. She knew she wasn't going back to that dungeon. But she definitely didn't have a key—she barely had any clothes. Shoeless, her bare feet felt like blocks of blue ice. She rubbed her arms, trying to dismiss some of the goosebumps, and knocked loudly on the door.

She waited and listened.

Nothing.

She knocked again, this time pounding long and hard with her fist.

Nothing.

A flush of anger crept up the back of her neck and, raw and immediate as the anger finally felt, it felt good. It felt very good. It felt powerful. Cass didn't try to fight it. Instead, she gave it free reign and, channeling months of confusion and frustration, she pounded again, hard enough to leave a dent, and shouted at the door: "I am the goddam Seer and I need to see what's behind this door!"

In response, as if she'd just said the magic words, the door popped free of its lock, loose on its well-oiled hinges.

Cass couldn't believe that had worked. She offered a verbal "Thanks" just in case someone was listening and pulled the door the rest of the way open. It opened onto a dark room. Instinctively, Cass leaned through and felt for a light switch. She found one, flipped it on, and the space was flooded with warm light. The room, with its modern furniture, shelves of books, and stainless steel appliances, was characterized by a tasteful but almost monastic sense of décor.

Surprised, Cass realized where she was. She was in Zach's apartment.

"What. The. Actual. Hell." Cass whispered to herself, trailing her fingers along the granite countertop.

"Zach?" she called out, hoping against hope that he would answer from the bedroom. But no one replied. Just to be sure, Cass poked her head into the bedroom. It was almost empty except for a low, neatly made bed. She had to give her head a hard shake to stop herself from picturing what it would have been like to spend the night there. To be sure she was alone, she looked in his closet and in the bathroom. Nothing. The apartment was empty.

Cass sat down on the couch in the living room, facing the wall of built-in bookshelves. Though no one was here, she also couldn't quite shake the feeling that, nonetheless, she wasn't *entirely* alone.

Cass leaned forward on the couch and massaged her temples with her thumbs. As she did, she noticed that a single book had been left out on the coffee table. It was a fat, tattered paperback with a painting of a desert scene on the cover: Frank Herbert's sci-fi classic, *Dune*. She picked it up and leafed through it and, as she did, she flashed on an extremely vivid image of Zach. He was lying in bed as a ten year-old, reading this book by flashlight long after he was supposed to be asleep.

Cass was so surprised by the memory that she dropped the book with a thud back onto the coffee table. After a moment's hesitation, she picked it up again and flashed on the same image—except, this time, she wasn't just an observer. She could *feel* what ten-year-old Zach was feeling. She could feel his rapt attention and sense of anticipation as he turned the pages. She could feel them as if they were her own feelings.

For Cass, this sensation was extraordinary—usually, even her own feelings didn't feel as if they were her own.

Cass set the book down, left the couch, and took a closer look at the overstuffed bookshelf. The range of books was enormous and eclectic but, slotted between a book on evolutionary biology and a thin volume of Walt Whitman poems, she found a high school yearbook. She flipped through the pages, smiling at the inscriptions and the occasional photo of a goofy, teenage Zach, until she came to a flower, pressed and dried between the pages.

When she touched it, she flashed on another memory. Zach was in high school. He and a girl had snuck out on a sunny spring afternoon. She twirled a wild flower between her fingers and slipped it playfully behind his ear. He looked like some kind of wood sprite. She tucked her hands inside the back pockets of Zach's jeans and pulled him close and kissed him. Surprised again, Cass could feel the girl's kiss, wet and full. Cass could taste her as if Zach's lips were her own. Zach slipped his hand under her shirt, soft against the flat of her stomach, and she laughed, pushed him away, and ran back into the building.

Cass snapped the yearbook shut and cleared her throat as if she, embarrassed, had just walked in on something. But even once she'd reshelved the book, she could still taste that kiss and feel the sun in her hair.

Cass left the bookshelf and wandered through the rest of room. She sat down at a worn wooden desk in the opposite corner. The top of the desk was clear and its simple design included only one flat drawer in the center. Cass hesitated for a moment and then pulled the drawer open. The only thing inside was a photograph. The image was facedown.

Cass stared at the back of the photo for a long time until, without thinking, she picked it up and flipped it over. It was a picture of her. She was the only thing in Zach's desk.

This object also came with a memory attached. She and Zach were sitting at a table in the coffeeshop after a late shift, preparing to close up for the night. They were the only ones there. Zach told a corny joke, smiled his goofy smile, and, despite herself, Cass laughed until she cried. She rested her head on the cool table top, trying to catch her breath. Zach parted the curtain of hair covering her face, looked her in the weak eye, and winked.

At this point, the memory turned itself inside out. Zach's memory bled into her own and she felt the whole thing from his perspective. She saw herself through his eyes. She felt what *he* was feeling sitting there with her, their friendship still new and uncertain. Zach was filled, from head to toe, with hope. He glowed with it, with the hope that he could charm her, with the hope that he could make her laugh, with the hope that he could look her in the eye and she wouldn't look away, with the hope that they might connect and that their connection might last.

Infused with Zach's sense of hope, Cass felt her own emotions, her own despair and hopelessness, recede within the normal bounds of human experience. She could still feel, directly and immediately, the complex cocktail of emotions swirling inside of her, but they no longer owned her. They no longer overwhelmed her. With a toehold in Zach's mind, she had some measure of control over her own.

When Zach leaned close and blew in her ear, Cass snapped back into the apartment and dropped the photograph on the desktop. She reached for the photo again, her hand hovering just above it, then touched it to slide it back into its place in the drawer.

But as soon as she touched it, the whole room started to grow brighter and brighter until the light engulfed her, saturating her, and the whole scene dissolved in a blinding flash of light.

34

WHEN THE LIGHT dimmed, Cass found herself laid out on the stone cold floor of her cell. Her bands were still broken but the unmarked door was shut.

Cass wasn't sure what time it was, but her cell seemed to be lighter now than it had been before. Some faint light still slanted in from the hall through the window in the door, but not enough to make a difference. She checked the opposite wall to see if light was coming through the window only to be reminded that, just as before, her cell didn't have a window.

Where, then, was the light coming from?

Though the floor was cold, Cass herself felt warm and strong and flexible. More, her head felt clear and her emotions, though immediate, felt channeled.

Effortlessly, she jumped to her feet from a sitting position and, in the process, noticed something unusual about her hand. She held her hand out in front of her, flexing the fingers. Her hand was radiating light, trailing wisps of white smoke as she waved it in the air.

"Huh," Cass said out loud. "I'll take it."

Cass felt along the edges of the handleless door, dug her fingers into the crack between the door and the jamb, and pulled. The door resisted but gave a few inches. Cass readjusted her grip for a better hold and pulled again. The heavy door groaned open, raising a cloud of dust, its hinges grinding like they hadn't been opened in a hundred years.

Cass stepped back and took a look at it.

"Huh," she said, echoing her earlier reaction to the light in her hand.

Cass shrugged and bolted down the narrow staircase into a hallway with a single bare bulb hanging from the ceiling. This time, instead of dead-ending, the hallway branched and then branched again. Each time, Cass chose the right. The third hallway funneled her into ascending a set of spiraling stone stairs that, through another dusty, groaning door, emptied into a room on the opposite end of the monastery's basement level.

It was a storage room of some kind. It wasn't lit, but Cass found that, by herself, she gave off enough light to make out what it contained. Taking inventory of the room's complement of lockers, racks, and tables, she found an array of weapons and uniforms, most of which looked like they were meant for someone the size of Dogen. But, on the table next to the door, she found exactly what she needed: her own jacket, shoes, and sword.

Cass slipped into her jacket and shoes, then un-sheathed her sword and sliced through the air with a couple of strokes. In her hand, the sword glowed white hot, trailing wisps of smoke just as her fingers had. She was tempted to write her name in the air with the light, like a kid with a sparkler on the Fourth of July, but she refrained. Instead, she held the sword at arm's length and watched it glow and smoke. The longer she stood still and focused her attention on it, the more calm and centered she felt.

"Huh," Cass said yet again, after a few minutes.

She sheathed her sword and slung it over her shoulder. It was time to go. It was time to confront Kumiko and find Miranda.

Cass slid through the door to the storage room and out into the hall. She could feel, in the soles of her feet, the whole building gently thrumming, like somewhere up above bass drums were being played and a mass of people had assembled.

Follow your feet, Jones, she thought to herself. *Follow the beat.*

Keeping to the inside of the wall, Cass silently made her way down the hallway toward the stairs leading to the upper levels. She had almost turned the final corner, when she heard a pair of loud footsteps coming her way. She doubled back a few yards and hid herself in a shadowy doorway. The guard turned the corner and immediately looked right at her.

Damn, thought Cass, *I forgot I was glowing like Christmas.*

Cass waved shyly at the guard and gave him a winning, apologetic smile.

He looked flattered and almost waved back before he remembered who she was. A look of panic replaced his aborted smile as he set about trying to wrestle his sword from the scabbard at his waist.

Before he knew what had happened, Cass drew her own sword in a blaze of light, took two running steps along the span of wall between them, and cartwheeled a crushing blow to the back of his head with the hilt of her sword. She landed on her feet like a cat. He crumpled to the floor, a ghostly wisp of smoke rising from the bruised spot on his head where the hilt of her sword had made contact.

Cass was going to have to use speed rather than stealth.

She flew up the stairs, drawn to the thrum, hoping to avoid anyone else. Fortunately, the halls were mostly empty. The beat grew stronger as she got closer. It drew her toward a large, ancient assembly hall at the center of the monastery's ground floor. Cass skirted the main entrance to the hall and doubled back to a flight of stairs that took her to an open deck with a railing that overlooked the assembly from the second story.

Cass sheathed her sword, crouched low, and—basically holding her breath—tried to pull the light in tight around her. She'd just have to hope that no one stumbled along or looked up this way.

From what she could see, she didn't think she'd have to worry.

All eyes faced forward. The assembly's attention was riveted on Kumiko as she stood, silenced the beating drums, and commanded the room with a glance. To Kumiko's right, a panel of Shield elders, men and women, stood convened. To Kumiko's left, Dogen had charge of Miranda, bound but unbowed. A fox lay at Kumiko's feet.

"The Shield is assembled," Kumiko intoned. A hush fell over the crowd. "And a panel of elders is convened in judgment."

Her small voice filled the room. Cass shifted uneasily in her crouch. Miranda stood with her eyes closed and back straight.

Kumiko continued. "The charge is simple but serious. Miranda Byrne stands accused of high treason. She has flagrantly and repeatedly violated her oath of loyalty to the Shield and disregarded her sacred responsibility to defend the world as we've received it from the monsters that would destroy it and remake it in their own image."

Kumiko paused, then appended a personal observation. "She has betrayed us. And given what she's been entrusted with, she is extraordinarily dangerous."

A mixed rumble of concern and approval passed through the crowd. The council of elders uniformly shook their heads in a gesture of censure and disappointment.

Seizing the moment, Miranda stepped forward, raised her head, and opened her eyes. She fixed the whole of the audience in her gaze and stole Kumiko's thunder. She was incandescent with anger and defiance, despite her powerlessness. Cass almost stood up in solidarity, but checked herself and hunkered deeper into her crouch.

"My friends," Miranda began, "I've loved you for many years. I've loved Kumiko like my own mother. But she is wrong. The Shield is stuck in the past, blinded by its prejudices, and bound by its own traditions."

Miranda rattled her chains for effect. Kumiko moved to take back the initiative, but Miranda forged ahead.

"We cannot return to the way things were. We cannot save the past. We can only work in the present to save the future. The moment for decisive, transformative action is upon us or all will be lost. You've been hiding from the truth for years!" Miranda's voice cracked with emotion.

The audience rumbled again, a murmur of surprise and incredulity washing through them. This wasn't going how they'd expected. Cass, on the other hand, wasn't sure what to think. She loved Miranda but she lacked the context she'd need to make sense of the bigger picture.

"Silence!" Kumiko commanded, addressing both Miranda and the audience. Her fox was primed for action.

Miranda turned to face Kumiko, tears streaming down her face, and addressed her in a low, quiet voice as if only the two of them were present. Miranda's voice, though, carried through the whole of the frozen room with a force unmatched by her previous exclamations.

"You're wrong, Kumiko," Miranda whispered. "You never believed in her. Her heart was too big. She scared you too much. If you'd had the courage to hang on to her, everything would be different now."

At this, Miranda shot a look straight at Cass on the balcony, meeting her eyes as if she'd know the whole time that Cass was there, watching and listening.

Is she talking about me? Cass wondered. *Was Kumiko frightened of me because I'm the Seer? Did Kumiko abandon me after my mother died?*

No one moved. No one breathed. Everyone waited for Kumiko.

"No," Kumiko said, wiping a single tear from the corner of her own eye. "I did what had to be done. I loved you both. And now, because of your shared recklessness, I've lost you both."

Kumiko's fox jumped up into her arms and she turned her back to the audience. She gestured for Dogen to take over.

"Council of Elders," Dogen called, "what is your verdict?"

The lead elder, a tall, thin woman in her fifties, stepped forward. She glanced at Kumiko, then at Miranda, then back to Dogen.

"We find Miranda Byrne guilty of high treason and —effective immediately—sentence her to death," she said.

35

THE SUN WAS up, streaming through the windows embedded in the upper level of the assembly hall.

Cass stood, the sun magnifying the light emanating from her, and shouted, "No!"

Every face in the room swiveled toward her.

With one step Cass leapt onto the balcony railing and with the next she propelled herself from it, launching herself across the room like a missile. In midair, she drew her sword. She landed with a somersault on the stage and directed all her momentum into a sword stroke that shattered the manacles that bound Miranda. Cass gathered herself and turned to the crowd. Both she and her sword glowed white hot in the full light of the morning sun, trailing wisps of smoke.

The crowd gasped. "The Seer," some murmured.

The elders cursed. Miranda rubbed her wrists. Dogen, absorbing the whole of Cass's flaming figure with a single, immovable glance, raised a wild eyebrow. Kumiko sighed and spun slowly back around, loosing her fox.

"Oh child," Kumiko said mournfully, "you don't know what you're doing."

"Neither, apparently, do you," Cass retorted, her sword raised, sensing there was some truth to both of their claims.

Miranda bared her teeth in a fierce smile. Guards rushed the stage. Dogen, moving with remarkable speed, grabbed for Miranda. Miranda's fingers danced, instinctively casting a spell that deflected Dogen's lunge with a shimmering green field while she jumped to the side, out of his grasp.

Cass caught all this out of the corner of her eye, but she didn't dare turn her attention away from Kumiko. Cass wasn't sure what to expect. The one thing she did know was that she couldn't give Kumiko any room to cast the spell that had laid her low last time.

Cass feinted high with her sword and then kicked low, sweeping Kumiko's left leg and sending her stumbling backward. Cass couldn't believe that had worked. Whatever else Kumiko might be, she wasn't, apparently, invincible.

Cass advanced on Kumiko but, almost before Cass could react to the unexpected success of her blow, Kumiko had planted her foot and regained her balance. Kumiko drew from between two pinched fingers the emerald specter of a katana and used it to parry Cass's second attack. Caught off guard by the ghostly green sword appearing out of thin air, Cass ended up on the defensive. She struggled to ward off a flurry of Kumiko's strikes that, with each deflected blow, nonetheless siphoned some of the heat and light from Cass.

Not good, thought Cass as she continued to retreat.

Kumiko advanced and Cass gave ground until she bumped into what she assumed was a wall. But it wasn't a wall. It was a Dogen.

Dogen looked over his shoulder at her with his typically bemused expression—Cass's head barely cleared his belt buckle—and swung a jug-sized fist at her head like he was swatting away a fly.

Cass ducked and Miranda took advantage of the distraction. Swinging her arm in three looping circles, Miranda drew a thin green cord out of the air and stretched the cord taut. She dove between Dogen's legs, looping the cord around his ankles, and then, as he began to topple, she looped it once more around his knees and twice more around his arms and torso. When he hit the ground, the floorboards buckled and splintered beneath his weight. Miranda tied the loop off, signaled for Cass to follow her, and then sprinted for the exit, dodging two more guards along the way.

But before Cass could follow, Kumiko struck her left shoulder with the green blade. Cass felt it pass right through both muscle and bone, crackling with an electric charge. Pain flashed through her shoulder and her left arm went limp and lifeless. Cass tried to scream but the blow had also knocked the breath out of her. All she could manage was a wheeze.

Cass wheeled around—short of breath and one armed—in an effort to keep Kumiko at bay.

"Dear girl," Kumiko tried again, "please stop. You truly don't understand the harm you're doing. Let me *help* you."

Again, Cass felt the truth in what Kumiko was saying. There *was* so much she didn't understand. But Cass also knew her ignorance wasn't the only thing in play. There was much more at stake than Kumiko was saying, maybe more than she knew.

While Cass tried to sort this out, Kumiko stood motionless, holding Cass's eyes with her own. Cass glanced at Dogen, still trussed on the floor and struggling against the glittering cord that bound him. At the same moment, from the opposite direction, Kumiko's fox launched itself at Cass's head. Cass caught sight of it out of the corner of her eye and, too late, flinched.

But the fox never reached her.

Atlantis intercepted the fox in midair and, in a ball of fur, the two of them tumbled off the stage and into the crowd, hissing and clawing and biting.

Kumiko struck again. Cass parried, guarding her limp arm. With some power still coursing through her, Cass could already feel her fingertips tingling, coming back to life, as the light counteracted the blow.

"Help me," Kumiko pressed. "Help me to protect the world we both love. Help me to protect the ancient traditions that your own mother died fighting for."

Cass wanted to believe her. But Miranda's earlier words echoed in her mind. This wasn't about traditions.

This wasn't about the past. In the end, this was about a hope for the future.

"Kibo," she whispered to herself, "kibo, kibo."

This was about hope.

It was about the hope that had anchored her mother's soul. It was about the hope that she'd found, everywhere she'd looked, tangible and immediate in Zach's mind. It was about the hope that he, from the start, had invested in her. Or, more truly, it was about the hope that he, from the start, had invested in the two of *them*.

"No," Cass said, hopeful, as time thickened and slowed around them, "we can't go back."

Cass attacked, forcing Kumiko onto her heels.

For everyone but the two of them, time had almost stopped. The rest of the room was filled with statues. Kumiko, though, seemed immune to the effect.

Still, as Cass continued to press her, Kumiko struggled to keep up. Playing on Cass's native turf, the drain on Kumiko's powers was enormous and her ghost blade began to weaken and flicker as she barely deflected Cass's continued blows until, with an enormous crash, Cass's final stroke shattered the spell and the blade.

Kumiko dropped to her knees, defenseless, with Cass's sword at her throat.

"We can't go back," Cass repeated, raising her sword ominously, "we can't go back."

Kumiko bowed her head and exposed her neck, indicating acceptance of her defeat. But, more than that, Cass sensed, the gesture indicated that, at least in part, Kumiko also accepted that Cass was right: they couldn't go back. There was, in Kumiko, still a spark of belief, a willingness to hope.

Cass hesitated.

The raised sword felt hot and heavy in her hand. But, teetering on the brink of a decision that she hadn't yet made, Cass was brought up short by the surprise of a quiet voice whispering in her ear.

"Cass," Zach said from behind her, one hand on her hip, the other gently restraining her arm, "stop."

36

CASS DROPPED HER sword with a clatter and, before Zach could react, spun around and wrapped him in a fierce hug. Startled, Zach waited a moment to see what would happen next. But when Cass pulled him even closer and squeezed him even tighter, he returned her embrace with a fierce relief of his own.

"Cass," Zach said, tucking her head under his chin, not letting go.

"I thought I'd lost you," Cass replied, finishing Zach's sentence for both of them.

"Never," Zach said as he pulled back to look her in the eye. Right away, he could tell that something had changed. He cocked an eyebrow and posed the question without needing to ask it out loud.

"Yeah, something's different. I took a little trip inside your head," Cass teased, tapping her finger against Zach's temple, "and I found a missing piece of myself . . . inside of you. Or, at least, I found a piece of you that I'm going to keep as part of me."

Zach arched his eyebrow a little higher, pulled Cass in close again, and tipped her backward with a serious kiss. The wisps of white hot smoke that had almost disappeared roared back to life and enveloped them both.

The kiss went on long enough that Kumiko felt compelled to interrupt them with a polite cough.

Cass started, immediately on the defensive as she began to reach down to recover her sword. Despite her raw, involuntary joy at seeing—and forgiving—Zach, she *had* just been fighting the leader of the Shield in order to save her aunt from a death sentence. Zach, however, just tried to compose himself, straightening his jacket and running his fingers through his still smoking hair.

But Kumiko did not appear ready to restart their fight. Instead, she sighed and shook her head, settling into a steely, determined demeanor as she straightened her back. As she did so, Cass realized that Kumiko was one of those people who stood taller in order to disguise the weight that leadership cast across their shoulders.

With a gesture of reverence and deference, Kumiko handed Cass back her sword.

Cass accepted it with a tiny bow, wary and confused as to exactly what had changed for everyone else.

"I am willing to acknowledge," Kumiko began, reluctant but resolute, "that your arrival has changed the dynamic significantly. The judgment rendered against Miranda will have to be suspended. We need to sit down together and begin again."

Cass nodded, grateful for the olive branch.

Kumiko took stock of the room. Most of it had cleared out in the commotion. "Miranda, however, is gone," she said, her voice tinged with disapproval as her attention fell on Dogen.

Dogen had just managed to free himself. He brushed off his pants, rubbed the back of his bruised head, and smiled sheepishly. Kumiko frowned in response. Cass and Zach shared a look, registering the subtle dynamic between the tiny woman and the mountain of a man.

The conversation, though, didn't have a chance to go any further. A monstrous crack of thunder shook the building and, visible through the balcony windows, a bank of dark, heavy clouds rolled over the mountain range, blotting out the morning sun. The assembly hall, brilliantly lit a moment before, was shrouded in darkness. The few flickering candles that remained only accentuated the contrast.

Cass reached for Zach's hand. The monastery bells begin to toll loudly and with more than a hint of panic.

"An alarm," Dogen rumbled, cracking his knuckles. "We are under attack. The Lost must truly be wild and desperate to come after us here."

As if in testimony to their wildness and desperation, the balcony windows shattered and a pair of feral vampires crashed into the room, teeth bared. Instinctively, Cass stepped protectively in front of Zach, sword raised, braced to meet them.

Cass, though, wouldn't need to handle them.

The pair of vampires had barely cleared the balcony and landed on the main floor of the assembly hall when they were greeted by Dogen.

With two giant strides Dogen bounded across the room, covering the thirty yards between him and the vampires. He grabbed one vampire by the head, the whole of its skull disappearing inside of his hand, and squeezed, the bones crunching audibly. Then he scooped up the remaining vampire with his other hand, banged the two of them together like he was playing with action figures, and impaled them both at the same time on an iron pole meant for displaying torches. They dissolved in a pile of white ash.

"Time to go," Dogen said, looking back over his shoulder. Cass, Zach, and Kumiko mechanically nodded their heads in agreement, their eyes wide.

"Yeah," Cass repeated, "right. Time to go." She still didn't trust Kumiko—it would take more than handing her sword back and a nicely phrased diplomatic olive branch to smooth over the fact that the woman had chained her up in a dungeon—but given the present options, Kumiko seemed like the more immediately safe choice.

"Yes," Kumiko said. "We must go. This attack is no coincidence. They are here for Miranda. We must find her before they do—or we may lose her forever."

37

DOGEN WAITED FOR them at the door to the assembly hall, scanning both directions for trouble. A handful of indeterminate screams and crashes sounded from elsewhere in the main building, but their immediate path was clear.

When they reached the door, Zach took the lead and they headed to the right. Cass was surprised at first but then realized that he'd probably spent years of his life here. For Zach, Kumiko and Dogen weren't strangers but mentors and allies. As they hurried down the hall, she couldn't help but see him differently against the opaque background of this unfamiliar part of his life. He was strong here, and decisive, and—following him around a corner—Cass also couldn't help but notice that he looked *amazing* in the tight black jeans he was wearing.

Focus, Jones! Cass thought. *You can't go around filled with light, indiscriminately responding with hope to every butt that wiggles in front of you!*

She had to get a grip. Miranda was the key. For the moment, Cass just needed to focus her hope and attention on Miranda.

"Cass!" Zach called, hauling her back into the present.

A vampire emerged from a side room and Cass ducked as he took a swing at her head. He missed. Cass punched him in the knee, crippling him for a moment, while Dogen backhanded him into the wall, crippling him for the foreseeable future.

They reached the end of the hallway without seeing any sign of Miranda. Zach waited for everyone to gather at the door with him, listening for sounds of movement on the far side. He pushed the door open and the four of them emerged from the main building and into the compound's central courtyard.

The courtyard was a melec. Rain poured down from black clouds. Lightning intermittently cracked in the sky. Bodies from both the Shield and the Lost were strewn about. Screams filled the air. And, even through the gusts of wind and pounding rain, Cass could detect the warm, copper scent of blood hovering amid it all. The stark reality of the stakes in this war were evident everywhere, even if Cass didn't understand what those stakes actually were.

Zach signaled the direction he wanted to go. Kumiko nodded agreement—the building at the far end of the courtyard offered the most direct access to the Underside. Zach counted backward from three with his fingers and they all took off sprinting across the court-yard.

Zach continued to lead the way. Dogen shielded Kumiko, hovering behind her with his bulk. Cass brought up the rear. However, halfway across the court-yard, Cass's forward momentum ground to a halt di-rectly in front of the ancient well that lay at the center of the entire compound.

Cass could feel something in the well calling to her.

She felt a deep, magnetic throb drawing her toward it. It pulsed, like a heart, with a regular rhythm. It pulsed like something deep inside of it was alive. For Cass, it felt like she'd been *recognized* as she'd tried to run past.

The rain fell even harder, plastering Cass's clothes to her body. She was soaked through. Just behind her, a Shield guard struggled with a feral vampire. Arrows whizzed all around, nocked and released from the guard towers that overlooked the courtyard.

Cass ignored it all. She stood there as if she were alone.

The well itself was wide, lined with stones, and cov-ered with a wood shingle roof. The roof was attached on both sides to a pair of tree trunks that straddled the well. The tree trunks were knotted, pruned of all but their main branches, and anchored deep in the ground by a massive root system that sprawled across the entire courtyard, interfering with row after neat row of cob-blestones. The trunks themselves twisted as they reached upward toward the rain and the sun.

Cass ran her hand along the smooth surface of one trunk and felt like she'd just plugged herself into an electric outlet. The force and clarity of the original pulse was magnified. It ran up her arm and straight into her head, obliterating the thought of anything other than the message it conveyed: "Come."

A stray arrow embedded itself in the trunk of the tree just above the spot where Cass had placed her hand, reverberating in the wood.

Realizing what had happened to Cass, Zach flew back across the courtyard to retrieve her, cursing himself for not recognizing the danger to her in advance. A vampire in a leather corset had crept up behind Cass. Zach arrived just in time to toss her over the side and down into the depths of the well. The woman screamed for a long time as she fell—though, ultimately, there was no audible splash indicating that she'd reached the bottom.

Zach peeled Cass's hand from the trunk of the tree, breaking the connection, and squeezed it. With his other hand, he turned Cass toward him, gave her a quick kiss on the lips, and said, "Come with me, Beautiful. We'll come back to this later."

Zach pulled her along with him toward the far end of the courtyard. The wind howled and the rain pounded. The farther they went, the more Cass returned to herself and the stronger her legs felt beneath her.

"What was *that*?" Cass asked when they stopped for a moment at the entrance to the second building.

"Miranda first, Cass," Zach urged, pushing through the door. "We just have to worry about Miranda first. There's a lot we'll have to sort through later."

"Right," Cass agreed, giving her head a shake to clear it. "Miranda first."

Dogen and Kumiko were waiting for them. This building, while old, was clearly newer than the first. As they worked their way deeper into the building, it became obvious to Cass that Zach had a particular destination in mind. There was someplace in particular where he expected they might find Miranda. However, as they rushed past a pair of large double doors that opened onto a massive library, Cass felt a tug that made her second guess him.

One of the doors to the library was slightly ajar.

"Zach," Cass said, reeling him back in, "I think she's in here."

Zach looked unsure but, as soon as Cass had said it, she felt the truth of it. Cass knew she was right.

Miranda was in there.

When Zach saw Cass's expression, he called Kumiko and Dogen back as well.

"Miranda is in here," he said, his voice conveying the confidence he had in Cass.

Together, the four of them pushed through the double doors and entered the library. The library was vast and labyrinthine and deep in shadow. Stack after stack of books receded into the darkness.

Only after their eyes had adjusted did they notice that the walls and ceiling of the library were crawling with Lost. And only after they realized this did they hear a voice that was recognizably Miranda's cry out in surprise, echoing indistinctly in the middle distance.

38

IF THERE WAS a pattern to how the library's stacks were laid out, it wasn't obvious to Cass. It seemed, instead, like the layout was meant as a test, a test designed to see if you were smart enough to find the book you wanted.

The opening rows of books were arranged in relation to the entrance as concentric circles radiating outward. At several points, both on the ends and in between, the stacks parted, allowing the patron to pass deeper into the maze. But these entry points never opened onto a single through-line that would take you from one end of the library to the other. Going deeper would always require a winding, wandering investment of time. In this sense, the library was designed as an architectural affront to anyone in a hurry. Wisdom, the architecture said, is only for the patient.

"Shit," Cass said, tapping her foot impatiently as she took in both the stacks and the feral Lost who'd infested them. "Shit, shit, *shit*."

The bigger problem was that they weren't looking for a book with a specific call number, they were looking for a person. And, unlike a book, Miranda wasn't going to stay put while they searched for her. As a result, Miranda was as likely to be found by someone who knew their way around the library as someone who didn't.

Kumiko took charge now, signaling that they should each take one of the four entrances. The more ground they could quickly cover, the better. They just had to not die while doing it.

Cass took the second opening from the left. She advanced quickly and quietly down the first row, her sword raised and ready. She took the first opening she found and wound deeper into the maze. Some of the shelves contained printed books, some contained leather bound manuscripts, and others contained scrolls and artifacts.

Cass hadn't gone very far when she saw a shadowy figure drop from the ceiling into the aisle one row over. She heard Zach cry out and a scuffle ensue. Zach was thrown against the shelves closest to Cass and they rocked backward, threatening to topple over, before settling back into place. Zach was pinned against the shelves, struggling to keep the vampire's fangs at arm's length.

Cass took a deep breath, closed her eyes, and plunged her sword through the stack, under Zach's arm, and into the vampire's heart. The vampire combusted in a shower of ash that left Zach coughing. He looked down to see the blade just inches from his own ribs, a copy of *Lady Chatterley's Lover* impaled on the end.

"You're welcome," Cass whispered as Zach pulled the book free and Cass withdrew the blade. Before Zach could say anything in response, Cass darted down her aisle, took the next opening, and left him standing there with the book open to page fifty-seven.

Zach tossed the book aside, waved away the cloud of ash, and continued. He hadn't gone more than two additional turns when he caught sight of Dogen's head bobbing above the neighboring stack, lumbering along. Even the faint light coming through the far windows was enough for Dogen's head to produce a tempting silhouette for their enemies.

Two Lost, crawling along the tops of the stacks from opposite directions, converged on Dogen's position. Dogen spotted the first one right away—the tops of the stacks were basically eye-level for him. But while he reached to snag the first one, the second leapt from behind, clearing two rows in one jump, and fastened itself with feral claws to Dogen's shoulders and back. Distracted by the attack from behind, Dogen missed his grab for the first and paid the price when it dodged his hand and slashed a deep, bloody line down the length of his arm.

"I'm coming, big guy," Zach said, scaling the stacks and swinging over the top. He lead with his feet, connecting squarely with the vampire draped around Dogen's shoulders, dislodging him. Free of that impediment, Dogen ripped the first from its perch on the shelves and swung it to the ground, beating it against the floor like a dirty rug. The vampire made a series of soft, squishy noises, then went silent. Dogen wheeled around, still holding the first body by the foot, and roared. Zach took the hint and dodged between his legs, out of the way, and Dogen wrapped things up by using the first one as a club for beating the second.

"Appreciate that," Dogen said, stepping over the bodies and continuing along his way.

Cass, meanwhile, was deep in the stacks, nearing the bay of windows along the west wall. She'd heard various scuffles unfold around the library but hadn't caught any sign of Miranda since the initial cry that drew them in. She'd almost come to the end of another row when a vampire in jeans, a black t-shirt, sunglasses, and a pair of short swords turned the corner. They came as close to bumping into each other –both of them startled—as is possible for two people with three swords.

"Shit!" Mr. Sunglasses yelped in a high pitched voice before he remembered that Cass was supposed to be afraid of *him*, not the other way around. He bared his teeth, trying to make up for his initial reaction. Cass bared her perfect teeth in return—four years of braces plus teeth whitening in high school—and the man, again, was brought up short.

There was very little room to maneuver in the aisle. Short strokes, lunges, and narrow parries were all they could manage. Cass had the longer blade, but Mr. Sunglasses had the advantage in height, strength, and number of weapons.

Cass went for his right arm, trying to draw blood and render that arm useless. Mr. Sunglasses, though, had some serious training—he'd probably been sword-fighting for hundreds of years—and turned the tables on Cass, slicing through her jeans and leaving a bloody nick on the inside of her thigh.

"You asshole!" Cass shot back, enjoying the felt immediacy of her own anger. "I work for minimum wage. How many favorite pairs of jeans do you think I've got?"

Before she could retaliate, though, a heavy book tinged with a faint green glow flew off the shelf next to Mr. Sunglasses's head, smashed into the side of his face, and knocked him sideways. His sunglasses went flying off.

Cass didn't know what to call him now.

The guy looked flustered. Just moments ago they'd been having a nice sword-fight and now all that was out the window. He wasn't sure how to defend himself against both Cass and the bookshelves. A second book flew off the opposite shelf, crashing into his knee, hobbling him. Then a third, fourth, and fifth book simultaneously launched themselves from the shelves, battering his head, stomach, and groin.

Cass took a couple steps back, giving—whatever this was—room to unfold.

Whole shelves were emptying themselves now, followed by the stack itself tilting and burying the bruised and stunned vampire. The upended stack, though, also had a domino effect and the two remaining rows that separated Cass from the bay of windows on the far side of the library also toppled over. The whole library echoed cacophonously with books falling and wood splintering.

As the dust settled, Kumiko peeked around the corner from one aisle back, with a mischievous smile on her face, her eyes glinting green.

"Uh, thanks," Cass managed. "And my wardrobe thanks you, too."

Cass seized the opening created by the downed stacks and, scaling the toppled structures, took the direct route to the windows. While they weren't going to sneak up on anyone after that racket, they could at least make up for lost time. Kumiko followed.

Once Cass had scrambled across the shelves and catapulted herself off the far end, she found herself in an open reading area with small groups of desks, lamps, and chairs. The bay of windows extended two-stories from the floor to the ceiling. The wind and rain pounded against the glass with enough force that Cass wondered how long they could bear the punishment. When another bolt of lightning lit up the sky, the glass rattled in response to the thunder and, with the whole room exposed in the flash of light, Cass could clearly see that she and Kumiko were *not* alone.

Toward the far end of this open space, a throng of Lost were gathered in a circle, heads bowed, all facing inward. Miranda and a hooded figure stood at the center, a respectful distance buffering them from the mass of teeth and claws gathered around them.

The hooded figure—the Heretic—was clearly in charge.

The figure was holding Miranda's hand—not gently and not violently, but firmly, commandingly. She leaned closer and whispered something in Miranda's ear. Miranda took it in, absorbing what she'd been told, silent and unmoving, suspended on the razor's edge of a decision.

Cass could barely breath. Her feet felt like cement blocks, like the shadows around her had reached out and pinned her in place.

Then the scales tipped, Miranda's face registered a decision, and she leaned toward the hooded figure and, in return, whispered something in their ear.

The Heretic drew back in a gesture that registered both regret and resignation.

"Are you sure?" the figure's powerful, strange voice asked, cracking.

"Yes," Miranda said, her resolve hardening around the sadness and anger displayed on her face. "Yes, I'm sure. I can't go back. This is the only way forward."

When the hooded figure wavered in response, Miranda snapped, "Now. Be quick."

Tugging the collar of her shirt out of the way, Miranda bared her pale, slender neck and the hooded figure, fangs glinting in a flash of lightning, sunk them into Miranda's throat.

"No . . ." Cass whispered, still unable to catch her breath or find the strength to move.

When the hooded figure withdrew, trails of blood from both puncture wounds streamed down Miranda's neck, soaking the front of her shirt. Miranda slumped. She wavered on the brink of losing her balance and collapsing to the floor. She looked, Cass thought, like she was about to die. But, at the last moment, her body stiffened and she brushed right past death's door to arrive at something else, at something that was neither life nor death. As her body stiffened, Miranda drew herself up to her full height. But she didn't stop there. With a visible surge, her body drew itself up taller than her full height, her shoulders now broader than their full breadth, her muscles now stronger than their full strength. With her hands clenched at her sides, Miranda threw back her head as if she intended to laugh but, instead, revealed her own razor sharp teeth.

Miranda was Lost.

"No!" Cass shouted again, this time finding her voice.

In response to that cry, the whole horde of Lost—some feral, some not—woke from the spell that had mesmerized them. Every head pivoted and every eye locked on Cass.

En masse, like a single viral body, they came for her.

39

CASS STARTED BACKING up. Almost immediately she bumped into Zach. He and Kumiko and Dogen were right there with her. They'd seen everything that she'd just seen.

There was no way to outrun the horde. They formed a tight circle, protecting each other's backs.

Kumiko took the point. Zach squeezed Cass's hand. Dogen rolled his head, cracking the vertebrae in his neck, and pounded his fists together.

Kumiko squeezed her eyes shut and tapped into a power that was even older and deeper than she was. She whispered a mantra to herself and a field of shimmering green light materialized around them. Zach and Dogen both followed suit, bracing the field with their hands, quietly repeating the mantra to themselves.

Cass readied herself, sword raised and glowing. The horde was almost on top of them.

But when the mass of them reached the protective shield, they simply flowed around it and past them.

Gathering their collective momentum, they rammed and shattered the bay wall of windows. Glass showered down around Cass and company, bouncing off the dome. The wind and rain poured in through the breach as the whole horde poured out into the raging darkness.

And then, just like that, they were gone. Miranda and the hooded figure were nowhere to be seen. And the four of them were alone in the library.

Cass didn't know whether to feel relieved or disappointed. She couldn't call what had just happened a victory. She would go to her grave with that image of Miranda, bloody and Lost, burned into her brain.

Cass slumped against the wall, sliding to the floor under the weight of it. Zach joined her, slipping his arm around her, pulling her close.

"I'm sorry, Cass," he said. "So sorry."

Cass buried her head in his shoulder. She didn't try to hide her tears.

Cass wasn't sure how long they sat like that. Kumiko and Dogen came and went. The monastery bells stopped sounding the alarm. The rain tapered off and the wind died down. But the longer they sat there together and the more willingly Cass let her grief wring her out, the more obvious it became to her that the spark of hope that had just ignited in her had *not* gone out. In some ways, in light of her grief, it burnt all the more fiercely, defiantly. Cass didn't know what was going to happen next, but she knew that none of this was over. She knew that this was just the beginning.

Eventually, Cass wiped away her tears and kissed Zach on the cheek.

"Thank you," she said.

"For what?" Zach asked.

"For hope."

Dogen came to collect them. The monastery was secure. Kumiko was waiting to see them.

Dogen lead them back to the main building, to Kumiko's own rooms on the highest floor. Cass and Zach were ushered into a Japanese style sitting room with paper walls and a low table. Kumiko was making tea.

While the water heated, Kumiko sat with them at the table. She gathered the silence around them for a few minutes and then began, her voice focused and formal.

"I have been alive now for more than four hundred years. The Shield was founded many thousands of years before that. Since its inception, it has been practicing magic, slowing things down, fighting to maintain balance and order, and preventing the world from destroying itself. This continues to be our mission, even today. We have taken sacred vows—unbreakable vows—to uphold it."

Zach and Dogen bowed their heads in reverent agreement. Cass could feel the weight that these vows had for them.

"But everything changed two thousand years ago with the first 'mutation.' Something happened to Judas. Something happened . . . *in* him when he betrayed the one he had willingly followed. Judas became cursed. He became lost. He became the first of the undead. And through him the curse began to spread across the face of the world and people began to be Lost."

Kumiko stood and retrieved their tea. As she skillfully poured it, it was obvious that the tea was scalding hot.

"I fear a rising tide," she continued. "I fear that we've reached a tipping point and that, if we do not proceed with immense caution, the whole world will be irreversibly flooded with this curse."

Cass picked up her fragile teacup, blew gently across the surface of the tea, and then held its warmth in her hands. Zach sat stone still. Dogen looked at his tea longingly, unable to wait. He downed it in one gulp, burning his tongue.

"Most of all I fear that their new leader will roll the dice with the future of humanity and entrust it to the Lost. I'm afraid that the Heretic will upset the fragile balance we've fought so hard to preserve, hoping against hope that being Lost may actually be a blessing rather than a curse."

Kumiko struck the table with her fist for emphasis, spilling her tea. "I *cannot* let this happen."

She paused, trying to calm herself.

"*We* cannot let this happen. As the Seer, Cassandra, you have been endowed with a rare gift. You wield rare powers. But these powers are also dangerous in their own way. After your mother died, I asked Miranda to watch over you. And then, several years ago, when

Miranda's loyalty to the Shield began to fray, I asked Zach to keep an eye on you both."

Cass looked from Kumiko to Zach. Zach sat still as a statue, his eyes fixed on his cup and saucer.

"You were not ready, Cassandra. But now you are. And because of Zach, you are safe and you are with us. Please, forgive him. Please forgive both of us. And please, above all, agree to join us in pulling this world back from the brink of annihilation."

Cass felt rooted and centered. She felt, for the first time in many years, as if she could, with time and patience, unchain the rest of what had been locked away inside of her all those years ago.

She reached for Zach's hand and squeezed it. He looked up from the table and met her eyes. Cass's weak eye wandered, but Zach was untroubled by it.

There was more to the story—perhaps much more —than Kumiko had just revealed. But she had to trust someone. And if she couldn't trust Zach, then who? At least for now, this was where she belonged.

"I'm in," Cass said, still looking at Zach rather than Kumiko. "I will be a sword for the Shield."

"Excellent," Kumiko replied, pleased. "In that case, I have an urgent mission for you."

40

THE VIEW FROM Richard's penthouse office in the York Tower was spectacular. The lights of London, hugging the curves of the Thames, twinkled seductively.

Richard leaned on his cane, his face nearly pressed to the glass. He was anxious for that day—soon his doctors said—when he could dispense with the cane and walk upright like a man. Given the scale of his injuries in the castle, his recovery had been miraculously quick. Being more than human certainly helped on that score. But, still, Richard found himself impatient. With all that was happening, this was no time to be on the sidelines.

"You have lived in London for hundreds of years," Maya said, pouring herself a shot of whiskey from Richard's bar. "There is nothing new to see out there."

Maya downed the shot in one go and poured herself another.

"On the contrary," Richard countered, his gaze still fixed on the city, "everything is new. Nothing is the same. The world has changed dramatically beneath our feet and the dust is far from settling."

Maya held up a second glass, offering Richard a drink.

Richard didn't turn around but admired her reflection in the window. They had worked together for a long time—from the beginning, really, for Maya. She was as striking as ever in her sleeveless dress, her hair loose to her waist. But he didn't feel the pull of desire for her. Whatever had once been between them had long since settled into the dependability of trust and friendship.

Richard shook his head slightly, declining the drink.

"Things could be worse," Maya continued. "We recovered the real chains of St. Paul and Paul's lost gospel. These relics will be valuable to us. More importantly, we kept these relics and their power out of the hands of the Lost, crippling their new leader's attempt to consolidate and control their numbers. We will have to think hard, now, about how to use that increasing instability to our advantage."

"Yes," Richard allowed, "this will have to be carefully considered."

Maya downed another shot, refilled both glasses, and wandered over to Richard, leaning against him. Richard put his arm around her and she nestled closer. She offered him another drink, but again he declined. Maya shrugged and took sips from both. She already knew what question was coming next.

"And Cassandra?" Richard asked.

Maya sighed.

"Of course. Cassandra Jones. She still understands very little. About herself. And about this new world she has wandered into."

Maya clinked the ice in her glass.

"She is working with the Shield now. Despite the debacle with Miranda, Kumiko successfully recruited her—in no small part due to the 'work' done by Zachary Riviera."

"Hmmm," Richard mused, frowning, "yes."

It was clear to Maya that they had moved on, now, from discussing geopolitics to something else. And she didn't care for it. She didn't like the fact that something other than logic and calculation were at stake. She didn't like how the worry lines radiating from the corners of Richard's eyes felt personal.

Maya pulled away from Richard, finished both their drinks, and set the glasses down on Richard's desk.

"She worries me, Richard," Maya said, forcing eye contact. "She worries me *about you*."

Richard nodded thoughtfully, sidestepping the argument.

"It's a delicate balance," he offered. "Cassandra is the Seer. Her powers are immense. We *need* her on our side."

"Right," Maya echoed skeptically, turning to go. "It is certainly true, at least, that you need her on *your* side."

Thank you for reading *Hopeless,* book 2 of A Vision of Vampires. If you enjoyed the book, please consider leaving a review on Amazon.com—your support is very much appreciated!

Sign up to find out about new books from Laura Legend, including *Blameless,* book 3 in *A Vision of Vampires:* www.smarturl.it/legendaries

Other Books by Laura Legend

Faithless: A Vision of Vampires 1

Blameless: A Vision of Vampires 3

Fearless: A Vision of Vampires 4

Contact information:

www.lauralegendwrites.com

facebook.com/lauralegendwrites/

laura@lauralegendwrites.com

Made in the USA
San Bernardino, CA
15 July 2019